MARTINI 1

To Dearie

R. T. Wiley

First Edition, 2016
Printed in the United States of America

Disclaimer

This is a work of fiction, a product of the author's imagination. Any resemblance or similarity to any actual events or persons, living or dead, is purely coincidental. Although the author and publisher have made every effort to ensure there are no errors, inaccuracies, omissions, or inconsistencies herein, any slights to people, places, or organizations are unintentional.

Cover photo courtesy of Fotolia.com
Cover and formatting by Debora Lewis, arenapublishing.org

ISBN-13: 978-1535233415
ISBN-10: 1535233419

MARTINI 1

R. T. WILEY

1

It was springtime in Seattle, and the weather was a mix. The trees and flowers were in full blossom and yet tomorrow there could be snow in the forecast.

Retired Seattle PD homicide detective Frank Martini was puzzled when industrial giant Marcus Radcliffe contacted his solo private investigator service. The Radcliffe's currently employed one of Seattle's best security firms to protect their business and residence, as well as provide a bodyguard for both Marcus and his wife Nadine.

Why did he need a personal investigator? The question nagged at him.

Martini leaned back in the creaking executive chair and propped both feet on the edge of his desk. Frank yawned and popped open a tepid can of Pepsi. A jolt of caffeine and sugar he thought, the essentials of a PIs diet. Frank was a laid back kind of guy, but he knew his business.

"What the hell, Marcus is a wealthy man. It certainly

wouldn't hurt to meet him, besides I don't have anything happening now anyway." Frank said aloud. This was the fourth year since Frank had started his PI business. There were seven other competing PI businesses in Seattle, and it was hard to crowd in and make a place for yourself in the PI world.

Having lived in Seattle all his life, Frank had heard rumors about M&N Biotec Inc. and the owners. He was aware that Nadine Radcliffe was a graduate of Washington University and held a doctorate in biotechnology. Nadine was in her mid-forties, he guessed, and Marcus was twenty years older. She was keenly intelligent, and in most circles, she'd certainly be considered a beautiful trophy wife. It was told she could be quite charming, yet she was also known to be the type who said what was on her mind.

Marcus Radcliffe had started his company four years before he met and then married Nadine. That had been ten years ago. They were strong-willed individuals who complemented each other within the company. The Radcliffe's lived in a gated estate that spread over twenty acres, landscaped with large trees and carefully manicured lawns. Oakwood Estates was located on the eastern outskirts of Seattle, a subdivision of twelve of the city's movers and shakers.

Martini remembered what he'd heard about Nadine's managerial style and laughed. He'd heard via the grapevine that the employees had coined several pet names for her: "Nasty Nadine" or "The Dragon Lady." They'd never dared say anything to her face: they'd lose their jobs. Furthermore, all employees had to sign an agreement forbidding any disclosure of company information or its classified secrets; they also endured a thorough background check prior to hiring.

And now, Radcliffe himself had called and requested a meeting with *him*, Frank Martini, PI, next Sunday evening at six. They were to meet at The Vapor Essence, an exclusive, private men's spa located in Seattle's downtown business district.

"I'll be in the steam room," Marcus had said on the phone. "My bodyguard and driver will stay in the car. It will be parked in the covered reserved section in back of the building. You should park on the street and use the front entrance. I'll leave your name at the front desk and let them know you'll be my guest." His tone suggested he was accustomed to getting his own way.

"I'll be there." Martini answered. *Whatever it involved would help pay next month's rent,* he supposed, *although he wondered what Marcus Radcliffe thought he could provide. After all,* he kept reminding himself, *Radcliffe already had his own security.* Strange.

Martini arrived at the club promptly and followed Marcus's instructions. The tall thin and muscular young man at the reception desk was a light-skinned African American. The knuckles on booth hands were large and calloused. Martini presumed that "Devon," according to his name badge, was involved in some sort of martial arts. Devon handed him a large white towel, a pair of flip-flops, and a key with a safety pin on it, then gestured toward the locker room without once speaking. Once inside the locker room, Frank removed his clothes, placed them neatly in the full-length locker, and closed it. Wrapping the towel around his waist, he tucked in one corner, and pinned the key to the towel. The flip-flops provided were too large, and he struggled to keep them from slipping off his feet. Shuffling and holding on to his towel, he reached for the door to the stream room and stepped inside. He could barely see through the steam; it was hot and oppressive. The heavy moisture stuck to his skin, searing him at first.

"Mr. Radcliffe, are you here?" Frank strained to see though the steam, wiping away water droplets that were condensing on his eyelids."

"Yes, Mr. Martini," Radcliffe answered in a matter of fact way. "Top row in the middle." Frank was wondering whether that was a seat of dominance as he climbed the steps and sat down beside Radcliffe. He hesitated to say anything in case anyone else was hiding in the thick steam. "Are we alone...?"

"We are alone." Radcliffe replied.

Martini continued looking around the steam room, searching. "Can we discuss why you've asked me here?"

"Yes, I'll get to the point, Mr. Martini. I'm quite concerned that my wife Nadine is conspiring to sell our company secrets, either to an individual or *individuals*." He emphasized the possibility of the plural.

Martini nodded. "But you have a security team, don't you?"

"I don't trust them. They may be closer to her than to me. I need someone from outside, such as you." He shrugged at this, wiping at the sweat trickling down his back.

"And I believe my wife has found herself a lover. That's of no real importance, unless she's conspiring to sell our secrets to that same person."

Frank Martini sighed. *Damn it was fiendishly hot in here. However, now Radcliffe had hinted at the crux of the matter, although he was claiming Nadine's affair didn't bother him.*

Marcus frowned, "I don't know if the information was being turned over to a foreign country, one of my competitors, or some individual. I want you to follow her and keep a record of everything she does. I want to know who she contacts and where she goes. I will expect pictures with times, dates, and a printed report. If you are able to record any conversations, all the better. Can you handle such an assignment?"

"Of course, that's all standard. Your request poses no problems." Martini said. "And I have the long-range equipment for the job."

"I'll pay whatever you ask. A package will arrive at your office tomorrow with cash up front for your services," Radcliffe said. "Do you own a smart phone, Mr. Martini?"

"Yes, sir, I do."

"Very well, what is your contact number?"

"I obviously don't have a business card under this towel. If I repeat it now, will you be able to remember it?"

"I have an outstanding memory, Mr. Martini."

Frank leaned in close to Radcliffe and whispered, as if someone might overhear.

Radcliffe repeated the number. "Is that correct?"

"Yes, sir."

"I will send you her picture and other information later this evening, along with a sizable amount of cash. Don't try to contact me. I will call you from time to time. Good bye, Mr. Martini." Signaling Frank with a wave of his hand, it was time to go.

Frank returned to the locker room and dressed. He went back to his shabby, two-room office on the third floor, turned on the overhead fan, and opened a window to let in fresh air. The office building had a fifty percent vacancy problem, maybe because the landlord lived-out of state, and didn't have much interest in his investment. After four years of barely getting by, Frank's business was financially holding its own. He never had such an important or wealthy client as Mr. Radcliffe.

If this job is successful there will be enough cash to upgrade my business and have a powerful reference for the future. Now, don't screw it up. Frank sighed out loud.

The next evening Frank was parked down the street from the Radcliffe's home waiting for Nadine in her black Mercedes to appear. It had been raining most of the day as it does in this part of the country. Frank had been in position less than an hour when the gate opened and Mrs. Radcliffe's car appeared. The car turned in his direction and was heading toward the city. As she passed, Frank could see that she had left her bodyguard behind. That in its self seemed odd. If she were up to no good, she surely wouldn't want a witness.

She drove to an elevated parking garage in the middle of the city and parked on the third level. Nadine walked to the service elevator, her high heels clicking on the concrete floor and echoing within the structure's interior. She stepped into the elevator and could tell immediately that someone had recently been smoking a cigar. She hated that smell; it reminded her of her grandfather's house when she was a kid and how she hated to go there because of the pungent odor. Nadine pushed the button for the ground floor and soon was out in the fresh air again. Frank had parked outside on the street and watched as she opened her umbrella and walked a half block to a beautifully decorated building and entered an up-scale restaurant. Canelo's was a popular restaurant, and there were people standing in line waiting for a table. Mrs. Radcliffe walked passed them and took a seat at a table that was already occupied by a very smartly dressed, beautiful Asian woman. The two women kissed on the cheek and exchanged pleasantries.

Frank got busy taking pictures of the chummy couple. When he was satisfied he had what he needed, he went back to the parking garage to write down Nadine's plate number in his handy notebook. He returned to his car and waited for two hours before getting concerned. His instinct told him to go back to the restaurant. When he returned the two ladies had disappeared, and Frank had no idea where. He knew Nadine had to eventually come back to her car, so he waited in the garage. She reappeared four hours later. She didn't look quite the same. She slipped into the car, adjusted the rear view mirror, brushed her hair, and added make-up. She then put on her safety belt and drove away.

Frank followed at a respectful distance as she wound through the city streets into a neighborhood of large old homes in an elite section of Seattle. The rain now was just a drizzle, and the sun had set. The darkness made it easier to follow her without being spotted.

Mrs. Radcliffe parked, got out of the car, opened her umbrella, and walked down the dark street. Martini parked a distance away and followed on foot.

The air felt heavy with humidity from the recent rain. It was late, and the only light was from sparsely placed street lamps. The streets glistened in the moonlight. Frank stood motionless in the shadows of the nearby trees, eighty feet back from the corner where Mrs. Radcliffe seemed to be waiting for someone. She was pacing back and forth.

From a distance, headlights broke the darkness and grew brighter as they came directly up to the curb where Mrs. Radcliffe was standing. The car stopped. The passenger-side window rolled down, but the car's interior was too dark for Frank to see inside. Mrs. Radcliffe took a few steps toward the stopped car and bent over slightly. Keeping the umbrella over her head, she leaned forward to talk with the person or persons inside. She reached inside the car with one hand. The flash from the muzzle inside the car was bright but not a sound was heard. She straightened up, turned, and began walking back toward her car. She came within ten feet of Frank without noticing him. He remained motionless in the shadows... After all, she had just shot someone and Frank didn't want to be her next target.

When she reached her car she looked both ways to see if anyone had witnessed what'd had taken place, when satisfied she got in and drove away slowly, thinking, *my part of the job is done.*

Frank walked quickly to where the car had stopped; the

engine was still running. He used his small flashlight to peer inside. A man was slumped over the steering wheel, looking back at him with dead eyes. One could see a dark spot in the middle of the dead man's forehead where the bullet had entered. A slight trickle of blood oozed out of the wound, ran downward, and settled in the corner of one eye. Frank reached into the dead man's jacket pocket and retrieved his identification. The passport gave the name of Wang Jun, a diplomat from China. He snapped a picture of it with his cell camera and one of the dead man, then wiped the passport clean before placing it back into Mr. Jun's jacket pocket. Frank was careful not to touch anything else and exited the scene immediately. He had no intentions of calling the police because he knew someone in the neighborhood would find the dead man and call 911.

Instead, he dialed Mr. Radcliffe and reported the evening's surveillance. Frank sent pictures of the other woman Nadine had met with and the dead guy.

"Do you recognize anyone?" Frank asked.

"No, neither one, but we have just begun," Radcliffe seemed quite sure of himself.

There was something in Radcliffe's voice that left Frank wondering if he was being truthful. It didn't seem to shake him that his wife had just killed a man. A man of importance: a Chinese Diplomat.

Nadine dialed a number. A voice answered and asked "Is it done?"

"Yes," Nadine answered.

"Was it quick and painless?"

"A bullet between the eyes at close range."

The person on the other end of line was named Yuke Jun, the wife of the now dead diplomat.

Frank sat at his desk in deep thought. The phone rang, jolting him out of his stupor.

"Martini here," he said with the phone halfway to his ear.

"Hi ya, Frankie boy," the voice on the other end said with a bad impression of John Wayne.

"Well, as I live and breathe… if it isn't my old partner at the PD, Tommy Salami."

Tommy's last name was really Saliman. He had picked up the nickname of Salami because if any of the guys were ever in the shower at the same time as Tommy, it made them look like they had just got out of a very cold-water pool. Tommy was a hulk of a man with hands the size of bear paws.

"Are ya keepin busy now days, like takin' pictures of cheatin' wives doin' the nasty?" Again he made with the bad John Wayne impression.

"Yeah, as a matter of fact I've hooked up with a very important client. I hope this is the one that will help me over the top. "What's on your mind, Tommy?"

"I've givin' my notice here at the PD, and I'll be pullin' the plug in thirty days. Thirty days. Where in hell has the time gone? Thirty years and it seems like just last week. Anyway, I was wondering if you had some part time work, now and then. Maybe I could be of some help." Tommy said.

"Tell ya what Tommy…, see if you can get your PI license, and I'm sure we can work something out."

"That's great Frankie..., I'll go to work on it right away. Talk to ya later partner," Tommy said with a smile in his voice as he hung up.

It was late. Frank walked over to the couch at the other end of his office and laid down. He was soon asleep.

2

Frank Martini wasn't married and didn't have any kids; that he knew of anyway. He liked the fact that he didn't have to answer to anyone but himself. Frank was 46 years old and he had given himself permission to sleep in his clothes, go several days without shaving or a couple days without bathing. Being alone he could fart or make those groaning sounds when taking a dump without offending a soul. He wasn't a heavy drinker and he had given up smoking twenty years ago. How he managed to stay at an even 175 pounds and look physically fit was a mystery. He ate poorly, hardly ever worked out, and only occasionally got a full night's rest. His idea of a vacation was to rent a shack down at the ocean, then lay in the sun with a six-pack cooler and watch the flat-bellied teenage girls with the skimpy pieces of cloth they called bathing suits. Every once in a while a woman of his approximate age would wander by and he would try to get lucky. Most of time he was successful, and most of the time they were bored housewives that wanted a little spark back in their lives. Frank would do his best to help them, and he never intended see them again.

He awoke as the sun was coming up to a cloudless sky. His apartment was a few blocks away from his office, so the walk in the early morning fresh air helped him gather his thoughts. His cell buzzed. It displayed the name Marcus Radcliffe.

"Yes, Mr. Radcliffe," Frank said rubbing his eyes.

"Nadine will be attending a three day seminar in Carmel, California. She will be staying at the La Vista Carmel, and will arrive on Friday and leave Sunday afternoon. I have made a reservation for you at the same location, for the full three days under the name of Roger Banister. If you don't have the appropriate attire, I have opened a charge account at the gentleman's clothing shop located on the ground floor of the hotel. I'm sure you will find your time will be filled with, shall we say, opportunity. Have fun, but do your work first." Marcus abruptly hung up.

Frank packed a few things and tossed in the equipment he was sure he would need. He took his car in for a tune-up and oil change; it too needed to be ready for the trip.

Marcus didn't mention how she would get there. No doubt Mrs. Radcliffe would be flying.

Frank punched in Tommy's number.

"Hey, buddy what's happening?" Tommy said.

"On the QT have you heard any conversation about some Chinese guy getting snuffed in the heights yesterday?" Frank asked.

"Na, not a word. Why?"

"Do me a favor – hang around the homicide dicks and see what you can pick up."

"Not a problem, partner," Tommy said and clicked off.

The mechanic who had been working on Frank's car came into the customer service area and told the employee at the desk that Frank's car was ready. He motioned to Frank to come to the desk, then recited all the points of the tune-up they performed, and went into a long list of recommended repairs they felt necessary. He thanked them, paid his bill, and walked out the door to the parking area where his car was waiting for him. He drove to a Mexican restaurant that he liked and had his usual lunch; a bottle of Budweiser, two soft tacos and an order of refried beans. As he sat there he wandered off into thought.

Maybe there's a light at the end of this tunnel after all. Ya know – I think I need a haircut and maybe a new pair of shoes.

Frank Googled La Vista Carmel on the Internet. According to the website it was a luxurious hotel right on the Pacific Ocean built in 1947 by a veteran of WWII, as a wedding present to his future wife. The hotel featured 85 guest rooms, private courtyards, library, lounge, several meeting rooms, secluded swimming pool, a lady's boutique, and a men's haberdashery. It was renovated in 1999, but still maintains its magical charm.

Not a place I could afford if my employer hadn't provided it for me.

Frank arrived at the hotel on Friday at 1:00 P.M. The man at the front desk let him know that check-in would be at 2:00 P.M. Noticing other guests in the lobby, Frank felt his very casual attire was better suited for the beach where he took his lazy vacations, rather than at this posh resort.

This was where the rich and famous gathered.

Frank walked down the hall away from the lobby carrying his bag. He passed a gift shop, a jewelry shop, and then he came to the gentlemen's store. The sign on the door read "Closed. Be back in ten minutes." The store manager walked up behind Frank and said, "I'm so sorry sir. I hope I haven't inconvenienced you long. I had to take a quick break." He unlocked the door and turned the sign from Closed to Open.

"May I be of service to you, sir?" The manager waved Frank into the store.

"Yes, I'm sure you can. My name is Roger Banister."

"Oh, Mr. Banister, we have an open account for you. I'm so happy to meet you, sir." The manager extended his hand as a gesture of friendship. Frank raised his hand and the manager grasped it with both hands and shook it briskly. Frank noticed the manager walked with a slight limp and spoke with a hint of an English accent.

"I will be staying here for the next three days, and I need the correct style of clothes in order to fit in with the crowd." Frank was feeling a little sheepish and had a grimace on his face, giving away the fact he was uncomfortable in this surrounding.

"I shall consider it a pleasure to fill your request." The manager took Frank by the left elbow and guided him to the shirt section.

For the next hour and a half the manager and Frank put together his complete three-day attire, in addition to a bathing suit, sandals, Hawaiian style shirt, and a large brim straw hat for the pool.

"Now all you will need is a drink with fruit on top and a little umbrella sticking out," the manager said, tipping his head and laughing. Frank quickly changed into one set of his new attire and stuffed his old clothes into a sack provided by the friendly manager.

After checking in at the front desk, Frank went straight to his room on the second floor, number 217, which overlooked the beautifully groomed grounds and pool area. As he viewed himself in the full-length mirror, he saw a new Frank Martini; clean-shaven, a trim haircut, and new expensive clothes. He smiled at the mirror and said aloud; "Time to go to work." He took the stairs down to the ground floor.

3

Frank walked into the large three-walled library room. On the right hand wall there were bookshelves from floor to ceiling filled with a variety of nondescript books. On the opposite end of the open entrance was a large old stone fireplace. Over the mantel hung an extremely large portrait of a woman dressed in a formal gown. The third wall was made up of two large stained glass windows. The large table in the center of the room was decorated with a variety of colorful fresh flowers. Name badges were neatly placed side by side in alphabetical order for the fifty attendees, along with a card listing the agenda for the weekend. A long stemmed rose in a small slender vase was in place for each lady. The West Coast League of Professional Women was about to get underway. Nadine's card was in the last row, Frank noted. There were additional agenda cards off to the side, and he helped himself to one. Frank wanted to know what time Mrs. Radcliffe would be involved with the group, and the time she would be on her own. He walked around the table to where he could get a good picture of all the badges and snap a few close-up shots, then walked out of the room and sat in a plush leather chair in the lobby where he had full view of the library room. Picking a magazine from the many that were on the coffee table in front of him. He pretended to skim through it while waiting for Mrs. Radcliffe to arrive and pick up her badge.

He took the agenda card out of his pocket and noticed that Nadine Radcliffe was listed as the main speaker on Saturday from eleven to twelve. He figured that would be the ideal time to place a listening device in her room and phone to record any conversations. If she used her cell while in her room, at least he would get a one-sided conversation.

I doubt if there will be a chance to place a bug on her person anyway.

Out of the corner of his eye he noticed a movement and quickly put the agenda card back in his pocket. It was a striking blonde lady who had taken a seat on the leather couch across from him. She was wearing a pale blue dress; her hair was pulled back into a ponytail. When she crossed her legs, her dress rose a little more and showed plenty of leg. Her left foot continued to rock back and forth as if she was keeping time to music. She caught him looking – however it didn't seem to bother her. She gave Frank a smile and turned her head, waving at another woman who had entered the lobby. The taxicabs were lining up outside, one after another with ladies dressed to a T. As they came into the lobby, they greeted each other with a handshake rather than hugs and air kisses.

It was light conversations with a business atmosphere but Frank had a hunch that might change after the cocktails began to flow later in the afternoon. Management had told him that there would be an open bar from five to six for the women's group. With their organization occupying fifty rooms and Frank's room making it fifty-one, that only left thirty-one rooms for any other guests. Frank had not seen any husbands in tow, so he assumed it was ladies weekend out. He had no way of knowing how many were married.

Maybe the boyfriends will show up later

The Asian woman he had seen with Mrs. Radcliffe a few days ago had checked in but didn't join the others. She went to the elevator and took it to the second floor. Minutes later, a Lincoln Town-car pulled up to the hotel. Nadine Radcliffe made her entrance. She was such a stunning woman. Everyone seemed to stop in their tracks just for a moment, their eyes following her to the front desk.

After checking in, she joined the rest of the ladies in the library to rousing applause. She smiled a friendly smile and thanked them. Soon some of the women headed to their rooms to freshen up while others gathered on the patio overlooking the beautiful gardens below. They had not seen each other for a year and had some catching-up to do. A few ordered ice tea, others wine. Within an hour the patio was empty. The ladies were gone and everything was quiet. Frank was quite sure they would reappear for dinner and cocktails later.

Through all the goings-on, the blonde across from Frank did not budge from her seat. Suddenly, she stood, walked over to where he was seated, and extended her hand. He stood and shook it.

"Please forgive this rowdy group; we only get together once a year for our annual meeting," she said with a warm smile.

"They're not what I would call rowdy by a long shot, Miss...?"

"Oh, my name is Diane – Diane Clark from San Diego."

"I'm Roger Banister from Allen Falls, Texas. Nice to meet you, Ms. Clark." Frank noticed she wasn't wearing a wedding ring on her long slender finger.

"Are you here alone, Mr. Banister?"

"Yes, I'm all alone, Ms. Clark."

"Why don't we just settle on Roger and Diane?" she said.

"Diane and Roger it is," Frank replied.

"Perhaps you could join me for a drink after dinner in the bar, say about seven o'clock?"

"It will be my pleasure," he smiled as she walked away.

This lady was certainly not like anyone I had ever dealt

with in my past. There had been some beautiful women, some intelligent women, some sexy women, but not like this one — she has it all. It looks as though I may be mixing pleasure with business. I think I know what Marcus Radcliffe meant when he mentioned opportunities.

Frank continued to browse the agenda card. The meeting would start tomorrow at 9:00 AM, break for an hour lunch, then continue at 1: 00 PM and adjourn at 4:00 PM. Sunday will start with a champagne brunch at 10:00 AM and election of new officers at 11:00 AM. The meeting will be adjourned at noon.

Frank went to the front desk and with a hundred dollar bill in hand and requested to see the guest register. Funny how the open guest register is left unattended for a couple of minutes and the employee disappears with the hundred in hand. He quickly scanned the Friday check-ins. There was only one Asian name listed, Yuke Jun, room 215.

Damn, that is right next to my room. How lucky can a guy be?

That means her room will have to be bugged, too. He went up to his room to set up and tested his equipment. It was 3:00 PM, and Frank had nothing on his schedule until 7 that evening. He decided to go lay by the pool and work on his tan.

It was a beautiful warm, sunny day with a light ocean breeze. Frank picked a lounge chair near the deep end of the pool and settled in. A young man with blonde wavy hair appeared. The kid looked like he was right out of a picture in a surfing magazine – dark tan, cargo shorts, open collared shirt, sandals and a pearly white, toothy smile.

"May I bring you a drink, sir?" he said in a tenor's voice.

"Yes, my good man, you can bring me two Bloody Marys."

"Will there be someone joining you, sir?" the young man asked.

"No, just thirsty," Frank looked out over the ocean. He remembered a time in the past when he was in the United States Marine Corps on a troop ship near Oceanside California, practicing disembarking down a large cargo net into a landing craft that bobbed like a ping pong ball in the water below.

But at this moment he felt as though he were in the lap of luxury; however, he also knew the bubble would burst sometime late Sunday afternoon. Frank tipped his hat down in order to shade his eyes and waited for his drinks to arrive. The sound of flip-flops coming closer got his attention. He knew it wasn't the young waiter with his drinks because he was wearing sandals, and they don't make any sound at all. Frank glanced up to see a woman he guessed to be in her mid-fifties. She picked a lounge chair next to his. She was very attractive and had a great figure. It was obvious she took pride in her appearance.

Not many women her age could get away with wearing a bikini and look good in it, but she does.

"Hello. May I join you?" she said in a soft voice.

"Yes, by all means, I would enjoy the company," Frank answered.

"Have you been poolside long?"

"About, ten minutes is all," He replied.

The young man returned with his drink order, and placed them on the tray table. Frank signed his room number. The young man asked the new arrival if she would care for a drink. She shook her head, and the waiter left. She looked at his two drinks, then at him. "Are you expecting someone?" she asked.

"No, just thirsty," he answered. She laughed politely.

"My name is Vivian Holster – my friends call me Vi," she said.

"I'm Roger Banister, my friends call me RB. Are you with the women's business group that I saw earlier?"

"Yes, I am. Why do you ask?"

"Oh, I was wondering what your organization is about?"

"We formed it ten years ago. Most of the members own their own businesses or are at least a C.E.O of the company they manage. All members are considered highly successful, and we are all type A Personalities," she said, and smiled.

"May I ask the name of your company?"

"Have you ever heard of Micro Dyne Dynamics?"

"I'm sorry, I haven't. I'm not much of a techy, I guess."

"Don't worry, most people haven't heard of it, unless they are in that field."

Frank had finished one of his Bloody Marys and had started on the second.

"What field are you in RB, if I can call you by your initials" Vi queried.

"I'm in the field of money," Frank said knowing that would spark a response.

"Money," she repeated with a questionable look. Frank sat up and stared her in the eyes.

"I suppose you really wonder why I say that."

"Yes, you can't just make a statement like that and not explain it." Her response was in a fun but demanding tone.

"Well, three years ago my dad bought a two-dollar power ball lottery ticket. It turned out he was the only winner. The payout after taxes was 40 million dollars. My mother had passed away two years before, and I'm an only child. Dad was in poor health. He gave me half the money and a year later he died. I inherited the other half. I quit my job as a civil engineer, have been traveling by myself since then, and enjoying life."

"Wow, what a great story, is it true? She asked.

"Absolutely true," Frank answered.

Vi rose from her lounge chair and looked down, "You're an interesting man, RB."

"Nice to meet you Vi," He tipped his hat.

"How long will you be staying, RB?" she asked.

"I'll be checking out Sunday afternoon."

"I hope we can talk again before then," she said.

"I'll look forward to it," as he tipped his hat again.

She gave Frank her room number 303, and mouthed the words, "Call me," then walked back toward the hotel.

Frank went to his room and ran an optical and audio camera line through the air conditioning vent near the ceiling and into the adjoining room's vent – room number 215. The equipment allowed him to see and hear everything in sight. The only area restricted from view was the bathroom.

"You are now mine, Ms. Yuke Jun," Frank whispered. He had brought several recorders to monitor the bugs he would be using. He thought of the dead diplomat and the name Jun, maybe he and Yuke were related. She knew Nadine, and Nadine shot and killed Mr. Wang Jun.

Frank showered and shaved for the second time. He wanted to be fresh for his meeting later at the bar with Diane Clark. When he finished getting ready, he still had time to kill before going downstairs to the bar. Frank had placed the camera's monitor on the hotel room's writing desk in his room and watched her. She was using the steam iron provided by the hotel to steam the wrinkles out of her clothes as she hung them up in the closet. She was wearing shorts and nothing else. He shut off the monitor knowing that it was still recording. Frank wasn't interested in her nudity; he wanted to hear any conversations between her and Nadine Radcliffe.

Frank's cell buzzed. The display showed it was Tommy Saliman.

"Hey Tommy, what's up?"

"Frankie boy, the Chinese guy you asked about was a diplomat, and the Chinese embassy is in an uproar. The dicks say they ain't got nothin' to go on. The Governor is giving the Chief seventy-two hours to come up with a credible lead or "Heads will roll.""

"Frankie, I know you probably won't tell me, but how in the hell did you know about this before anyone else?"

"Yeah, you're right Tommy. I'm not going to tell you, and you keep your trap shut. We'll talk later."

4

Whenk Frank entered the cocktail lounge, one couple occupied the two seats at the far end of the bar. The rest of the patrons were from the professional women's group. Diane was seated with three other ladies. She noticed Frank right away and almost sprang from her chair. It was like she was laying claim to him before anyone else could. He couldn't help note Diane's very tight canary yellow and black, cross back bandage dress that made it appear she was in commando mode. Her clothes were form-fitting and very high end. As he looked around, he saw many of the other ladies with a similar look, but she stood out from the crowd. She put her arms around Frank's neck and drew him in close as if they were old friends.

"Roger, I'm glad to see you could make it," she purred in his ear.

"I was counting the minutes," he said.

"There are only a few empty tables left." She took his hand and guided him to the nearest one. A perky little waitress appeared dressed in a maid's outfit to take their drink order. Diane ordered a Long Island Ice Tea and Frank requested a Vodka Martini.

He saw Nadine Radcliffe with a crowd around her, but the Asian woman was nowhere in sight; maybe she would be here later, he mused.

"Diane, how long have you belonged to this group?"

"This is my third annual meeting," she said rather proudly.

"Do you come to the La Vista Carmel often?" she asked.

"First time for me, but I have a feeling I will enjoy my stay here this weekend."

"Oh, I'm sure you will Roger," she placed her hand on his and gave it a squeeze.

A four-piece band made its way to the corner of the room and set up their instruments. Six handsome men walked into the lounge; they all looked to be from 25 to 30 years old. You could hear the cougars growl, as the men were snapped up by the first six ladies to reach them. Vi Holster was sitting on a barstool and caught his eye. She waved and smiled then walked to where Diane and Frank were seated, leaned over, and whispered in his ear.

"Have a wonderful time tonight, but tomorrow night you belong to me," she said. Then she walked away swaying from side to side.

"You obviously have met Vi Holster already," Diane said.

"Yes, this afternoon we met at the pool."

"She's a classy lady, and I'm sure you will enjoy her company tomorrow," Diane said.

"What is it with your group and the men here?" Frank mused.

"We all have an understanding. When we find an unattached male and we want his company, we can only spend one night with him. The next night, another member of our group has an opportunity to bed him," she explained.

"Wow, I think I hit the lottery again," Frank replied grinning.

"Some of the ladies prefer to hire escorts for the weekend. Those are the men that just walked in. A few women are unattached lesbians hoping to find first timers that are bi-curious. Quite a mix, huh?" Diane said.

"It's enough to consider this place for an annual stop," Frank said.

"We all work very hard. For many of us, this is our only vacation, so we make the most of it."

The band begin to play, soft slow dance music. Back when Frank was a cop he dated a ballroom dance instructor. She had schooled him in Fox Trot, Cha-Cha, Waltz, and the Swing. The music that was playing was what you would call, "The Sway" – just hold each other close and sway in time with the music. He knew his way around the dance floor pretty well.

Frank stood and asked Diane if she would dance with him. She rose from her chair, grasped his outstretched hand, and walked to the dance floor. He pulled her close, feeling her ample breasts press against his chest. Other couples joined them on the dance floor. The older ladies with the young male escorts were digging their fingers into the young escort's butts. Frank wanted to be a gentleman. Diane was a beautiful lady; he didn't want to have sex with her. He wanted to make love with her. He sensed that is what she wanted also.

He wanted to know more about the ladies organization, and the gentlemanly approach would render more information – of that he was sure. As they danced, he kept his eye on Mrs. Radcliffe. She was certainly the queen bee of the group.

"This morning when we met in the lobby, that lady standing over there had walked past us and into the library to a rousing applause. Is she someone special?" Frank asked.

"That is Nadine Radcliffe, the founder and leader of our organization."

"Oh.., I noticed she hasn't picked a male companion."

"She's married, but rumors has it she also likes the ladies. You seem very interested in our group."

"Only because it has such strange rules concerning the evening agenda," Frank quipped.

"We started out with three members, two have died. We allow up to seven new members to join each year by invitation only. Not every person can meet the test," Diane said.

"Test, what test?"

"Sorry, I can't go there. We are sworn to secrecy," she said and smiled.

"He bent his head down and kissed her neck and whispered, "Maybe I'm a spy."

"I doubt that – who would want to spy on a bunch of over-the-hill horny women?" she said.

"Maybe you should tell me why you're here this week end?" Diane asked.

"To tell you the truth, it was on my bucket list." Frank went on to tell her the lottery winning story.

"For real?" she exclaimed.

Frank put his hand to his heart and said, "On my mother's grave."

"Sorry mom"

"Are you married?" she asked.

"No, never really got around to that," Frank answered.

"Let's go to my room and you can fill me in on all your travels and other things," she said leading him off the dance floor.

They took the elevator to the third floor. Arm in arm they walked past the noisy ice machine and to room 311. Diane called room service and ordered champagne.

After it arrived she walked into the bathroom, took her clothes off, and got in the shower. She called out, "Roger, please join me." There was a knock on the door. It was the bellman with the champagne. Who put it in ice and left two glasses. Frank signed Diane's name on the tab and slipped him a twenty, and the bellman left. He went into the bathroom, removed his clothes, and stepped into the shower with her. They kissed long passionate kisses and explored each other's bodies. After a complete cleansing, they stepped out of the shower, dried each other off, and put on the two terrycloth robes that were hanging on a hook behind the door. Diane found a romantic music channel on the TV and turned the lights down. Frank uncorked the champagne and filled the two glasses.

"A toast to new acquaintances," she said. Their glasses clinked, and they moved closer together. She was the first to drop her robe. Her naked body was so beautiful it took his breath away. He then followed by letting his robe fall to the floor. Frank slowly lowered Diane onto the cool sheets of the bed. For the next hour they took their time fondling, kissing, and probing each other. Frank worked his way down and tasted Diane's sweet juices. Then it was her turn to please him. She brought him to the peak and stopped, just long enough for him to cool down.

"I want you inside me, Roger," Diane said softly. He slid on top of her, reached down and placed his hands under her legs, raising them up and putting them over his shoulders. His hard shaft slowly entered her awaiting wetness. When they each were completely satisfied, Frank got up and poured two glasses of cold champagne.

"Wouldn't this be the time we would each light up a cigarette, if we smoked?" he said laughing. She joined him in laughter.

"It's getting late. I have a business meeting in the morning my dear, so I'm going to kick you out now. I had a great time this evening. Thank you for being such a gentleman."

Frank drew her close and kissed her again. "Same time next year?" he asked.

"It's a date," She answered. They smiled at each other, and he left.

Maybe by next year I will be finished with this job, have a flourishing business, and can afford this place on my own. Then I will be able to tell her my real name and the reason I'm here.

5

Frank went straight to his room feeling very satisfied. His work tomorrow would start when Mrs. Radcliffe was giving her speech. Frank took off his clothes and got in the shower again. He let the warm water cascade down his body. With his eyes shut he visualized all that had taken place in the last two hours. He grabbed the soap and lathered himself completely. After rinsing off he dried himself with the large towel supplied by the hotel. He wrapped the towel around his waist and tucked it in. He walked into the bedroom, sat down at his desk, and flipped on the video and sound from next door. He hit the rewind button and sat back and watched. No movement or sound appeared on the screen. He hit the forward button until the time on the machine showed ten minutes after nine. Yuke entered the room and came into view. She was on her cell phone.

"Yes, yes, of course I will… have I ever failed you?" Yuke asked. She listened for a moment, then said, "I will call you as soon as I have something to report." She listened again. "Thank you, General Chang," she said bowing as if he was in the room with her and then clicked off.

There was a knock on her door. She looked through the peephole and saw Nadine Radcliffe. She opened the door, "Please come in," Yuke said politely. Nadine walked in carrying a bottle of Red Label Scotch and twirling a pair of black panties around her finger.

"I can't stay too long because I have a speech to give in the morning. So, girl let's get it on," Nadine said. She quickly slipped out of her top and pulled Yuke toward her.

Frank didn't think he wanted to watch what was about to take place between the two women. He turned off the screen monitor and would listen to the audio in the morning, in case there was something concerning Nadine's business.

Frank was up Saturday at 5:00 AM. He had showered and completed his normal hygiene routine, then went downstairs to the hotel restaurant for breakfast. There were three other people all sitting separately when he arrived, and none of them were ladies from the West Coast Professional Business Women. Frank picked up the morning paper and began to read. He felt a tap on his shoulder. He turned and saw Vi's smiling face.

"Good morning, Roger," she said.

"Vi, and a good morning to you," he replied standing up.

"May I join you?"

"I would be delighted, Vi," he answered. He pulled out her chair and they both sat down.

She was dressed in fashionable jogging attire.

"I have just finished my morning run," she said.

How in the hell does she do it? She had finished her run, not a hint of her make-up running, not a hair out of place, and she still smelled wonderful.

"How far do you run?" Frank asked.

"Two miles every morning. And when I'm home, I go to the fitness center for an hour."

"No wonder you are in such great shape."

"Thank you. I try," she said with a smile.

Their order came and they ate. When finished, she tapped her lips with her napkin, stood and kissed Frank on the cheek.

"I'll be expecting you at 8:00 P.M, my dear man. I will order our drinks after you arrive," she said. She waved her hand, then blew him a kiss as she was leaving. He picked up the check for breakfast, looking around to see if anyone noticed her display of affection. Frank took his paper and went back to his room. He needed to get his mind focused on what he was sent here to do. Frank reviewed the video from the next room, listening for anything in their conversation that might incriminate Nadine. Nothing of any use during the entire time the two ladies were together.

Maybe old Marcus is barking up the wrong tree, and his

wife isn't selling company secrets after all.

It was edging toward ten o'clock. His plan was to enter Nadine's room, search for any incriminating evidence, and then plant the bugs.

He slipped the electronic master key into his pocket. It was programmed to open any hotel room that required an electronic key-card. He knew the ladies' program began at nine o'clock and he wasn't sure Mrs. Radcliffe had left her room. Frank had to be sure, so he went down to the lobby and checked the signboard that offered information on events of the day. The professional woman's group was listed as meeting in the Tulip room at 9:00 AM. Frank looked at the hotel information map and found the Tulip room. He hoped he could somehow get a peek inside to make sure Nadine was attending. The hotel staff was going into the Tulip room pushing a coffee cart. While the doors were open, Frank got a look at the head table and Nadine was there. He turned and headed for her room on the third floor. Housekeeping had their cleaning carts in the hallway and were busily at work.

He entered her room and placed the DND sign on the outside handle. Nadine was a very neat person, even the used linens were neatly folded and made ready for the maid service. Frank checked her closet and the clothes that hung there. Then he concentrated on her cosmetic bag and the one large luggage bag. He noticed the airline tag strapped around the handle from

Alaskan Airlines. He opened the suitcase and found a copy of her flight information. He took a notepad from his pocket and wrote down the return flight information. He knew if she had any secret company information, it wouldn't be left in her room.

Working quickly, Frank put the bugs in place. He opened the door and retrieved the DND sign, placing it back on the inside door handle. He checked the hallway – no one was in sight. Frank headed for the stairs that would take him down to the second floor. When he got there the hallway was completely empty of hotel staff and guests. Arriving at his room, he turned on the recorder for the bugs in Mrs. Radcliffe's room. He could hear the air conditioner humming in the background and knew the bugs were working properly.

The ladies group would be breaking for lunch at noon. According to their agenda, lunch would be served on the patio outside their meeting room. Frank noticed there was a balcony at the end of the third floor hall. It wasn't so much a balcony as it was a platform for a fire escape. From that spot he could easily watch the ladies group during lunch without being seen--- or so he thought.

Frank took his binoculars out of the case and waited. As the noon hour approached he made his way out to the platform. He wanted to observe Mrs. Radcliffe's actions. While he was waiting for the ladies to break for lunch, he called Tommy Saliman.

"Yeah," Tommy answered.

"Tommy, it's Frank Martini..., are you busy Sunday afternoon?"

"Na, not really. What can I do for ya,"

"There's a woman flying into Sea-Tac on Alaska Airlines Sunday afternoon, flight number 2215, due in at 6:10 PM. Can you tail her until she gets to her home? I'm not sure if someone will be picking her up or if she drove her Mercedes to the airport. Go early and check the VIP parking area. Her plate number is UBI-689, and don't let her see you. There is a C-Note in it for you," Frank said.

"I always like easy money. Consider it done, my friend," They hung up.

Frank knew he had to wait until early Sunday afternoon when Mrs. Radcliffe would check out before he could retrieve the bugs from her room.

Tonight would be the ladies last night for fun and frolicking. Tomorrow morning they would meet for the election of new officers and plan next year's annual meeting. After that Mrs. Radcliffe would check out, head for the airport, and be home by 7 PM.

Frank had to drive back to Seattle. That would take him about fourteen hours behind the wheel with a stop in Eugene, Oregon, where he would spend the night to break up the long drive.

6

Frank knew it probably would be a waste of time watching the luncheon, but one never knew for sure. When the ladies went back into the meeting they would be there until 3:00 PM. He went back to his room, put on the earphones, and listened to Yuke's room. All was quiet. He wondered where she might be hiding.

He had time to kill and thought a dip in the pool would be nice.

Frank put on his swimsuit, flowered shirt, sandals and straw hat. He grabbed his sunglasses and headed for the pool.

He picked a lounge chair, took off everything except his swimming trunks, and dove in. The sun was warm and the water was cool. He began swimming laps slow and easy. He couldn't believe that on such a beautiful day he was the only person using the pool.

When he stopped and stood in the shallow end, the pool boy asked for his drink order.

"Two Bloody Marys, sir?" the young man asked.

"Yes, wait about ten minutes before you bring them," Frank said, shading his eyes from the sun.

"Very good, sir," he turned and left.

Frank continued his laps until he was exhausted.

Damn, I could really get used to this sort of lifestyle.

Frank stepped out of the pool and was using a large towel to dry off when he heard a voice from behind him say.

"What are you up to, Mr. Banister?" Frank was surprised to see Vivian Holster standing there.

"Well, hello Vi. I didn't think we would be getting together until later this evening,"

Frank said looking like he had just been trapped... like a deer in headlights.

"I cut away from the meeting just for a few minutes to ask you about the balcony scene."

"What are you talking about, Vi"

"Cut the bullshit, Roger, or whatever your name is. I saw you on the fire escape earlier, using binoculars to watch us. You had better come clean or I'm going to sic the hotel manager on your ass. I'll report you as a peeping Tom."

"Hold on Vi – you got it all wrong," Frank said

"This better be good," she warned him.

Frank was thinking as fast as he could to come up with a believable story and trying his best to maintain his smile.

"Okay, let me explain. Last night after I left Diane's

room, I went down to the bar. There were only a few people there, and one was from your group. We had a few drinks and we started playing truth or dare. I won the first round, and dared her to flash one of her boobs right there in the bar. She did a quick pull down of her tube top. She won the second round and she dared me to go into the ladies bathroom and pee in one of the stalls with the stall door left open. I did, and was lucky that no one saw me. We decided to do one more dare and she lost."

"So what was the dare?" Vi said with hint of a smile.

"She agreed to go commando at your meeting today and she had to prove it by flashing me, while I was on the balcony," Frank said laughing.

"Who was this lady, and I use the term lady loosely?" Vi asked.

"That I can't and won't tell you." Now they were both laughing.

"You're an ass. I'll see you tonight but no truth or dares," she said and walked away, as the pool boy walked up with his drinks.

He took a big gulp of his drink, rubbed his hand across his forehead, put on his straw hat, and sat down. *Whew that was a close one.*

Frank gathered up his things and went back to his room again. The women's conference would be finished in an hour. Frank showered and changed into his eveningwear. He took the stairs down to the main level and walked to the lobby area. He sat in the same seat he'd sat in before. From his vantage point he could see whoever walked into either the lounge or the dining room. He picked up the daily paper and actually began to read, glancing up when he saw movement in the area. The front desk was quiet, the clerk looked as though she was filling out some sort of report. A man approached the front desk and asked for Mrs. Radcliffe's room number.

I'm sorry sir, we are not allowed to give out that information." She had a sweet and pleasant voice. The man asked the hotel clerk to call Mrs. Radcliffe's room and tell her he would like to talk with her about "Juke Box." This was a code name for a top-secret project. The man had a manila envelope tucked under his arm. He had government written all over him – neatly pressed dark suit, white shirt, black tie, black shoes highly shined, and a close-cropped hair cut. He seemed out of place at the beach resort. *Frank wondered what he wanted with Nadine Radcliffe.*

The clerk said, "Mrs. Radcliffe will meet you in the library right over there," the clerk said pointing to the open ended room across the hall. "She will be down in five minutes," the clerk continued. The clerk went about her work. The man walked over to the library and waited. Nadine was right on time. They exchanged pleasantries and the man handed Nadine the envelope. She opened it and laid it on the large table. Nadine was reading and signing page after page. When she had finished, the man produced another envelope and Nadine placed the signed paperwork inside the second envelope, sealed it, and gave it to the man. He thanked her and he left. Frank was taking mental notes of what had just taken place. Nadine placed her copy in the other envelope and left for her room.

Perhaps, Mr. Radcliffe would understand when he heard about it. And what the hell is The Juke Box?

Frank was watching the monitor in his room when he heard someone knocking at the door, but it wasn't his door it was Yuke's room next door. She answered and greeted Nadine.

"When will you be leaving?" Nadine asked.

"In the morning. My flight time is 8:45 AM on United Airlines."

"Oh, you'll get home before I will," Nadine said.

Nadine sat down in a chair next to the bed and looked up at Yuke.

"Are you going to let me spend the night with you?" Nadine asked.

"I was hoping you would," she replied.

"Let's have dinner in the room tonight by candlelight, and I'll order a bottle of Red Label. There are a couple of things I need to discuss with you, but it can wait till later." She stood and kissed Yuke on the lips. "I'll see you at seven," she turned and left. Yuke seemed puzzled, shrugged her shoulders and disappeared into the bathroom.

"*Finally, maybe I'll find out what these two are up to besides sex. I will have eyes and ears on them, while I'm enjoying myself with Vi Holster.*"

7

It was nearing 8:00 PM and Frank was at Vi's door with a small arrangement of flowers. He knocked and said, "Room service." She opened the door. "And I mean service in the most respectful way." Frank handed her the flowers. Vi smiled, and asked him in.

"You are such a rascal," she said. She pinched his butt as he passed her on his way into the room.

Frank was surprised to see that she had a suite with a Jacuzzi bubbling away. The lights were low, and music was playing softly in the background. There were lit candles placed around the room for effect and incense was burning, adding to the romantic atmosphere. She was wearing a long, loose flowing maxi-dress and nothing else. He could smell her perfume lingering in the air as she passed by. She reached into the ice bucket and handed the bottle to Frank. "Would you be so kind to do the honors and open it?" *Pop!* The cork was removed and Frank poured the champagne into the two glasses. She stood in front of him and slowly unbuttoned his shirt and let it slide to the floor. Frank's hands cradled her cheeks and kissed her softly. Her hands were undoing his belt. She fumbled with the button on his shorts and they, too, fell to the floor. All that was left were his speedo and his sandals. Frank's hands had lowered to her waist and was gathering up the material of her long dress inch by inch until it was up to her waist. She took hold and pulled it over her head. Frank stepped back, admiring her tan body.

Frank's package was restricted but was growing of its own accord.

He pulled down his speedo and his shaft sprang out like a jack-in-the-box.

"Not yet my handsome lover," she purred. "Let's take our champagne and slip into the Jacuzzi, where we can get to know each other a little more.

They settled into the hot bubbling water and were drinking, touching, and kissing.

Frank had his share of women in his life, and Vi was close to being the oldest, but her class, grace, and beauty surpassed the rest. She had a charm and warmth about her that would rival most others. Ten minutes had passed when she said, "RB how would you like a nice sensual massage with stimulating oils?"

Tell me what man could refuse an offer like that.

They each emerged from the Jacuzzi. She had retrieved a large bath towel from the bathroom and spread it on the king size bed. She wrapped a smaller one around her waist and asked Frank to lie down on the bed. He laid on his stomach with his hands above his head and turned his head to the right, so he was looking away from her. Vi climbed onto the bed and straddled him. Frank closed his eyes and waited. She leaned over him, rubbing the oils lightly over the entire back of his body.

Frank heard what sounded like a grunt and felt the full weight of her body collapse on him then slide off unto the floor. He sat up and called her name. She wasn't moving and seemed to be unconscious. Frank immediately gave mouth-to-mouth resuscitation with no response. He checked her pulse and couldn't find any. He put his ear to her chest and listened for a heartbeat All was quiet.

He grabbed his phone and started to dial 911, then hesitated. *I can't be involved with this!* He used the room phone and dialed Diane Clark's room. When she answered, he told her to come to room 303. He told her it was an emergency and come alone. She tried to ask something, but he had hung up. He got dressed in a hurry and washed the two champagne glasses. Three minutes had passed, and there was a knock on the door. Frank opened it and ushered Diane in. She had been getting ready for bed and didn't have her face on. Funny, how different women look without their make-up.

"What the hell is going on?" Diane wanted to know.

"It's, Vi, I think she had a heart attack and is dead."

"What!" Diane said with a startled look. "Where is she?"

"Right over here on the other side of the bed," Frank answered in a whisper.

Frank and Diane walked over to where Vi lay nude and motionless.

"Did she die while you were having sex?" Diane wanted to know.

"No, she was giving me a massage… we hadn't had sex at all."

"Why did you call me?"

"Because you knew that Vi and I had a date for tonight and if I had just left her here, to be found in the morning, you would have thought I had something to do with her death – and I didn't!" Frank stared down at Vi. Even in death she was an exceptionally beautiful woman.

"You believe me, don't you?" Frank asked.

"Yes, Roger, I do. Did you know she was married?" Diane said softly.

"No, she never mentioned it."

"We have to clean this place up before we call anyone. The family doesn't need to know about her little indiscretions. She has been married for forty years you know."

"I had no idea. How old was she?"

"I believe she turned 62 last week. She was talking about it yesterday at our meeting.

"Damn, I thought she was more like 52."

They picked her body up and laid her on the bed. Diane was struggling to put Vi's maxi-dress back on her limp body. When she had finished, Diane arranged Vi's body in a natural pose. They both looked at her and were saddened.

Frank shut off the Jacuzzi and dumped the Champagne. Diane put the bottles of oil in Vi's luggage and removed the large bath towel from the bed, returning it to the bathroom. Frank's eyes searched the room, spotted the incense, and flushed it down the toilet. Next he gathered up the candles and put them in the wastebasket. He checked the room again.

"Now what?" Diane was looking blankly into the bathroom mirror.

"We need to get the hell out of here," Frank said and walked toward the door. We'll just let the maid find her in the morning." Diane nodded with tears were streaming down her face. They both left and Frank wiped the door handle on both sides and closed it behind him.

Frank hurried back to his room and didn't encounter anyone in the hallways. He went to his room refrigerator and took out the flask of whiskey he had brought with him on this trip. He took a large tug on it and sat down on the edge of the bed. His first thoughts were to pick up his stuff and head back to Seattle, but as an ex-cop he knew better. If there were an investigation of her death it would make him look suspicious – and he didn't want to deal with that.

Frank was watching his monitor as Nadine came back to see Yuke. The digital time showed it was 7:10 PM, and they were sitting down for dinner. The bottle of scotch was half gone when she sat back and asked Nadine what it is that she wanted to talk about. "It's about our arrangement," Nadine said.

"What about it?"

"You know how I feel about you and would do anything for you."

"Yes, I feel the same way," Yuke answered.

"What was the real reason you wanted me to kill your husband? I know you said he was cruel to you, but I think there is more to it than that."

Yuke looked down at the floor. "You are a very perceptive woman Nadine." There was a couple reasons I needed him out of my life. As you are aware, we want the plans to the Green Light program, and the new one called Abilene Gray. My husband and I work for the Chinese government, as you know. He was to turn both programs over to them, and we would receive a bonus of ten thousand American dollars – and no doubt a medal of some kind. With him out of the way, you and I could sell it to the highest bidder on the open market. We would make millions on each one of the programs. Then I would fulfill my end of our arrangement and kill your husband. After that we would disappear before anyone figured it out."

The ladies stood and embraced each other and kissed long passionate kisses before collapsing on the bed.

Frank sat there with his mouth open and couldn't believe his ears. "Wow," he said aloud. He shut the monitor down before it had finished.

Wait until Mr. Radcliffe sees this!

Frank called Marcus on his cell number. It was late and a sleepy voice answered. "Hello, Mr. Radcliffe. "Frank Martini here, I have gathered some information for you. Will you be able to meet with me on Tuesday morning about 10:00 AM at my office?"

"I'll be there," Radcliffe said.

"In the meantime I would suggest you be extra cautious, as I have information there will be an attempt on your life at any time."

"What!" Radcliffe said.

"I'm sorry for the late call sir, but I thought it necessary to inform you of what I have uncovered." Marcus Radcliffe listened intently, "I will heed your help and advice, Mr. Martini. In the meantime, I will be gone on a two-day trip and meet you at your office on Tuesday at 10:00 AM" The two men clicked off.

8

Sunday morning Frank was up early, listening to last evening's recording again. Frank decided when he arrived back home he would transfer everything onto a disk, so Mr. Radcliffe could watch and hear what had taken place. Frank had his day planned. When Nadine checked out he would retrieve his electronic bugs from her room as well as Yuke's. After that he would pack up his gear, check out of the hotel, fill his car with gas, and then head for home. Frank finished his daily grooming and headed to the hotel restaurant. He ordered eggs over easy, a fruit bowl, toast and coffee. Diane walked into the dining room, dressed smartly in business attire, and sat at the table next to Frank. They didn't speak at first.

Finally Diane whispered, "Good morning, Roger."

"I hope it is," Frank whispered back.

"Housekeeping is starting their rounds about now," she said in a low voice.

"Check out is at 11:00 AM, so it won't be long now before her body is discovered," Frank whispered.

"Our meeting starts at ten. Vi will be noticeably absent. I'm sure someone will call her room and when there isn't any answer, they will go to check on her," Diane said.

"Will you be flying to San Diego?" Frank was trying to change the subject. He could see it was upsetting Diane, and she was ready to break down.

"Yes, my flight is scheduled for 1:25 this afternoon."

"Where will you be going next Roger?"

"I'm heading for the Grand Canyon for a four day rafting trip. Then I'm headed to Cabo San Lucas, Mexico, to do some Marlin fishing. I have two friends that will be meeting me there."

Damn, I'm getting good at making up stories on the spur of the moment.

From where Frank and Diane were setting, they could see through the double doors into the main hallway. Two maids rushed past the dining room's double doors and a third trailed behind. When the maids reached the front desk they were out of eyesight, but it was easy to hear them speaking excitedly in Spanish to whomever was at the desk. Within minutes the fire rescue squad had pulled up at the front entrance with their red and blue alternating flashers. Four firemen hurried into the hotel carrying their heavy, life-saving gear and disappeared down the hallway to the elevator.

"Diane, you Nadine, and Vi were all on the same

floor, right?" he asked. Diane nodded.

Nadine had left Yuke's room and was about to enter her own room when the firemen nearly knocked her over rushing by.

A maid was holding the door open for the firemen as they entered single file. Her pale body was lying on the bed just as Diane had left her. The firemen checked Vi's vitals. They immediately found she was in rigor mortis. One of the firemen called dispatch and requested the medical examiner. He also requested the police send someone, as a matter of routine procedure.

The ladies group had gathered in their meeting room, talking and laughing amongst themselves as they awaited the start of the days meeting. Many had heard the sirens, but they had no idea what all the fuss was about at the hotel's entry. Soon they could hear the elevator doors open and saw paramedic crew followed by the medical examiner walking toward the main entrance pushing a gurney carrying a body zipped tightly in a body bag. Suddenly the room became quiet. The manager walked into the room where the ladies had gathered for their meeting and asked for Nadine Radcliffe. Nadine raised her hand. The manager approached her and whispered something in her ear, he turned and left. Nadine walked to the podium and said, "Let me end the rumors and speculation. Our dear friend Vi Holster has passed away due to a heart attack.

I will notify her family. She will be fondly remembered by all of us. Could we please have a moment of silence on her behalf?" Each of the members bowed their head and a few sobs were heard. No more than a minute passed when Nadine brought the meeting to order and began with the agenda.

Frank walked up the metal steps in the stairwell, his shoes making a hollow, echoing sound that seemed to bounce off the concrete walls. When he reached the third floor, he eased the door open that led to the hallway and peered out. The maids were busy with their work, popping in and out of the various rooms. He stopped in front of Nadine's room and noticed a DND sign hanging on the handle. Using his master key he quickly slipped inside, but left the sign on the door in place. Nadine had already packed and was ready to depart as soon as her meeting was over. Her cell phone was setting on top of her luggage. On the bed she had placed a sealed envelope addressed to the maids, no doubt a hefty tip was inside. She was a classy lady, while also being an adulteress and a murderer.

Frank picked up her phone and dumped its information into his phone, hoping there was additional information that would be of use to Mr. Radcliffe. Frank removed the two bugs he had planted in the room and put a tiny one into Nadine's phone, then left her room. Frank walked past Vi's room. He had a hard time understanding how a woman like Vi, who seemed to be in such good physical condition, could have a heart attack. He felt a pang of guilt as he continued walking toward the stairwell. Before he entered, he looked up and saw a security camera.

How dumb of me not to think of that until now. The only time the hotel security would review the camera is if there had been a problem. Dying of a natural cause is not a problem; it's an act of nature. The camera tape is probably on a 24-hour loop and erases its self every twenty four hours.

He was sure the medical examiner would find her death to be of a natural cause. Frank entered his room. When he was satisfied all of his equipment was accounted for he packed it and took the suitcase down to his car, placed it in the trunk, and locked it. On his way back inside he saw Diane settling up at the front desk. They exchanged glances, and he winked. Diane smiled and tipped her head as if to say, "See you next year."

9

Tommy stopped at the VIP parking gate and flashed his badge to gain entrance to the airport's elite parking area. The sky was cloudy and threatened rain at any moment. Tommy was driving an older, unmarked Chevy sedan. It didn't look like it belonged among the Cadillacs, Mercedes Benzes, Jaguars, and other expensive cars. The lot was nearly full. Tommy drove slowly down the rows of the covered parking. He looked at the small card he was holding in one hand while driving with the other. The card had Nadine's license plate number on it along with the make and color of her car. He stopped, turned his head to the left. "There it is – right make, right color," he whispered to himself. Tommy glanced down at the card again and read the card out loud – UBI-689.

He left the VIP lot and parked a short distance away and waited. He was sure she would be taken to her car by the airport shuttle service. Tommy wanted to get a good look at her before she got into her car, and in order to do that he would have to use his binoculars sitting on the seat beside him.

The city is paying me, and Frankie boy will be hitting me with some easy cash. I like this double dipping stuff. He smiled and patted the steering wheel.

The weather closed in and the rain started; slowly at first, then it came down in sheets as the wind increased. Tommy wondered if the weather would delay Mrs. Radcliffe's flight from landing. He drove around to the cellphone lot and read the board on incoming flights. Alaskan flight 2215 was showing it was on time and would be touching down in twenty minutes. He drove back to where he had parked before and waited patiently. The wind had died down but the rain was still heavy. In this weather it would be difficult for Tommy to get a good look at her.

Thirty minutes had gone by when a small shuttle bus pulled up in front of Nadine's car. The driver got out, opened an umbrella, and waited for his passenger. A woman appeared from the shuttle with a scarf over her head and the collar of her jacket pulled up. The dutiful driver put the umbrella over Nadine's head and tried his best to keep her dry while she walked over and got into her car. He remained there for a minute and eagerly accepted her tip. The driver returned to the shuttle and drove away.

Nadine exited the VIP parking with her lights on and her windshield wipers on high. Tommy slid down in his seat so as not to be seen. After she passed, he sat back up and turned the key to start his car. The only sound he heard was, *click, click, click.* "What the hell!" he shouted aloud. He tried it again and got the same results. He pulled the hood latch, got out, raised the hood, and looked at the engine. Tommy was about the furthest thing from an auto mechanic that there was. He grabbed the battery cable and it came off in his hand.

"Shit," he said out loud.

He put the cable back on the battery post and twisted it back and forth trying to get the cable clamp tight. He pulled out his gun and checked to make sure the safety was on, then began beating the cable connection on the battery post with the butt of his gun to make sure it was as tight as it could be. When he was satisfied, he put his gun back in its holster, shut the hood, and got back in the car. He was completely soaked. He had been cursing the whole time. Tommy took a deep breath and turned the key and the engine came to life. It was too late to complete his assigned task. Mrs. Radcliffe was nowhere in sight, and he was clueless where she had gone.

Money down the drain--- just because of a faulty cable connection. *Oh well, shit happens, as they say.* Tommy drove to the exit, paid his toll, and headed for home. The rain had stopped and the sun was peeking out from behind the clouds. Perhaps the rest of his evening would brighten up also.

Frank Martini had carefully packed his bags, paying close attention to the new wardrobe he had gained while staying at La Vista Carmel. For his trip home he would wear the same clothes he had arrived in; they felt comfortable and familiar. His bubble of luxury had burst, and now it was time to get back to reality.

Frank picked up the morning paper at the front desk while checking out. He noticed the article regarding a woman that suffered a fatal heart attack while attending a woman's conference at the La Vista Carmel Hotel. The rest of the story was brief and to the point, giving Vi's accomplishments, age, and information about her family. It saddened Frank to think about the whole ordeal. It appeared the medical examiner ruled it a death by natural causes.

Frank opened the door to his car and wondered if he would ever see Diane Clark again. If she found out who he really was, would she still be attracted to him? Or even more would she believe his story about Vi's death? Diane's image filled his mind as he pulled onto the highway heading north. It was Sunday, and he felt the traffic would probably be light. His thoughts turned to Nadine and Yuke and then to Marcus Radcliffe. Maybe with the new bug in Nadine's phone, it would yield the information Marcus Radcliffe was seeking.

The miles clicked away. He noticed the roadway sign advertising a fast food stop at the next exit. He glanced at his watch and realized it was 1:30 in the afternoon.

He pulled up to Curley's Curbside Cafe.

I've always wondered how new business owners pick the name for their businesses. Some take a lot of time and put real thought into it, and others, well, you wonder. I remember a sign I saw in Utah, it read, "One mile ahead, Eat at Joe's and get gas. Not a lot of thought went into that one.

Frank drove into a parking place at Curley's and went inside. It looked clean enough and the place was about half full. If you check out the bathroom and if it's clean, chances are the kitchen is too.

Two men entered the cafe and sat down at the booth behind where Frank was sitting. Frank ordered the all American meal – hamburger loaded, fries, and a soft drink. He could hear the men giving their orders to the waitress who was behind him. "Just water for now," one man said. The other asked for coffee, black, no sugar.

Frank finished and paid the waitress at the register. He told her he would like to pay the bill for the two men who sat behind him.

"You know them?" she asked.

"No, not really, but they seem like such nice fellas." He turned and left.

Frank got back on the highway and headed north. He was sure the two guys were from the government. Two miles down the road Frank pulled off the highway again and turned right onto a county road that lead to nowhere in particular. Within minutes a black, four-door sedan pulled off the same ramp, and also turned right. Frank knew they apparently had a tracking device planted on his car. He pulled into a driveway of a farmhouse and drove to the back so it would be hard for anyone to see his car from the road. He jumped out and went to the back end of the vehicle and quickly found the magnetic device attached to the frame. He walked over to the farmer's tractor and put the devise under the metal seat. He got back into his car and headed to the highway. The Feds car passed him going toward the signal and didn't pay any attention to him. Frank headed north again at a higher rate of speed. He was sure he could put enough distance between him and the Feds while they were sitting on the transmitting signal waiting for it to move again.

Why in the hell are they tailing me? Was it because of Nadine? or was it Yuke? or maybe her husband? Marcus wouldn't have any reason to sic the Feds on me.

10

He drove northeast until he reached Interstate 5, then followed it north and crossed into Oregon. The sign showed Eugene was two hundred miles ahead. When Frank reached Eugene, he planned on spending the night. He would use cash for his motel and gas so the Feds couldn't follow credit card purchases.

He called Tommy to see how things went with him.

"Hey Tommy, did you follow Mrs. Radcliffe home?" Frank asked.

"Aw, no it didn't work out that way," he said sheepishly. Tommy went on to explain the problem.

"Shit happens," Frank said. "Can you set on her house the rest of the night?"

"Yeah, I guess so – can I still earn the C note?" Tommy asked.

"Sure Tommy – not all is lost."

"I feel bad about losing her in the rain the way I did."

"If she doesn't come out by midnight, call it off. She no doubt is in for the night. I'll check in with you tomorrow," Frank said. They clicked off.

The suits know where I live and where my office is. They know I know they are there. Why plant a tracking device on my car? What the hell is going on?

Frank took the off ramp to Downtown Eugene. He drove until he saw a Holiday Inn and found a parking place near the entrance. The young lady behind the counter gave him a room on the first floor near the end.

"You're invited to the morning breakfast. It starts at 7:00 AM." She handed him his change and a receipt for his cash purchase.

He went back out to his car and brought in the recordings he had made at the La Vista Carmel Hotel. Frank set up the recordings, both audio and video, in sequence for Mr. Radcliffe's viewing. After that task had been completed he headed for the hotel dining room. There were a few couples already enjoying their meal when he was seated.

The waitress took his order and left the table. His thoughts returned to Diane and Vi. Thoughts that were both exciting and sad at the same time. He was looking down into his water glass when his meal arrived and snapped him out of his trance. A man walked into the dining room. He was ushered to a table close to Frank. The man was younger then Frank, dressed in a black suit and white shirt with a close-cropped haircut.

Every time Frank looked up the man seemed to be staring at him. He finished his meal, paid the check, and walked to the nearest restroom. Frank figured if the guy was going to make his move, he would do it now. Frank stood in front of the sink and large mirror. Seconds went by and the young man came into the restroom, stood at the sink next to Frank and asked, "Are you Frank Martini?" Frank glanced up with an angry look and charged the guy, pinning him against a metal stall wall with his forearm pushing hard on the guy's neck. The man's face was instantly flush red.

"Yes, I'm Frank Martini. Who in hell are you?" The man coughing, croaked, "I'm David Gilbert. My sister is Sue Lynn Gilbert. You saved her life when she was taken hostage ten years ago in Seattle when you were on the police force." David Gilbert regained his footing and rubbed his throat. "I never had a chance to thank you for your actions back then."

"Oh God, I'm so sorry," Frank muttered. I'm on a case right now; I thought you were one of the guys following me," he said, brushing the man's lapel. David spoke awkwardly, "It's okay. I guess this is an odd way of trying to introduce myself. Just wanted to thank you." Adjusting his clothes, he reached out his hand and Frank shook it.

Frank asked, "How is your sister doing now?"

"Actually, very well – happily married; has a beautiful young daughter and a good life."

Standing taller, Frank said, "That's great. Tell her I said hello."

"I will," David said, turning and walking rapidly away. Frank retreated to his room and took a shower.

Maybe the shower will clear my head, and I will stop acting like a fool. I'm seeing bogeymen everywhere, and that's not like me.

After breakfast the next morning, Monday, Frank hit the road, figuring to be back home by evening. He looked forward to the meetings with Radcliffe and with Tommy.

—◆◆◆◆—

Tommy had less than two weeks until his retirement. As a short-timer, the department doesn't really give a hoot about what he does during this time. He's given an address to check out or a phone call to make for them – just busy work. That leaves Tommy with a lot of free time. He knows he could use it to make some extra cash.

—◆◆◆◆—

Four agents from the FBI were parked in front of the security gate at Yuke's home shortly after she arrived from her trip to Carmel on Sunday afternoon. The agents tried to contact her by phone and on the speaker box located at the security gate. There wasn't any response. Yuke knew they wanted to question her about her husband's murder and her whereabouts for the last several days. They knew their options were limited, with her husband being a diplomat. His diplomatic status extended to his family. The FBI left several messages but they remained unanswered.

Her late husband had told her that their property was off-limits to all U.S police agencies and government officials. She knew the only person she could safely contact without raising suspicion was Nadine Radcliffe.

A black limo with blacked-out windows drove to Yuke's gate and waited for it to open. The gate remained closed. The four FBI agents stood by, looking quizzically at the limo as it backed up and drove away.

She peered out her window, watched the scene, and recognized the limo. It belonged to General Chang. She shuddered with her hands clenched. When her phone rang she began to shake and cry, unable to control her emotions. Cautiously, she put her trembling, pale hand on the receiver and waited.. She knew the unidentified caller was General Chang, so she let it ring and ring – she had no desire to speak with him. He would want to know if they had made any progress in obtaining secrets from Nadine's biotech company and to question her about her husband's death. Yuke knew that if she wasn't forthcoming with answers, Chang would resort to torturing her. That was his reputation.

Nadine's cell buzzed. The display showed it was Yuke. On the fourth ring she answered.

"Nice to hear your voice," Nadine said sternly. Are you ready to complete your side of our bargain?"

Yuke explained what was happening outside her home. "I have no idea how in hell to get out of here," she whispered, as if the Feds could hear her.

"Don't worry – I will figure something out. I'll call you later," Nadine hung up.

11

Marcus wasn't home when Nadine arrived from the airport. He hadn't left her a note or a message of any kind as to where he might be. Her mind turned back to Yuke's situation. She decided to send one of her bodyguards to pick her up and bring her back to Nadine's house.

She instructed her man to hide Yuke in the trunk of the car, out of sight of any preying eyes. If anyone were still at Yuke's gate, it would be easy to see if the driver was alone in the car when it left. Nadine called Yuke and told her the plan, and also told her to bring her gate remote so she could get back in at a later time.

Nadine dialed Marcus's cell number. He answered on the third ring.

"Where are you love?" she asked.

"I decided to take in some scenery while you were gone. I'm in Portland, Oregon, right now, looking for a famous lighthouse."

"When do think you will be back home?"

"Perhaps late Tuesday afternoon," Marcus responded.

"Okay, you be safe sweetheart," she said and hung up.

That is why I'm staying away from you and whatever you are planning, my dear dragon-lady.

Marcus was really at a motel in Spokane, Washington, packing up and heading back to Seattle for his Tuesday morning meeting at 8:00 AM with Frank Martini.

The bodyguard arrived with Yuke in the trunk and pulled into the open garage. Nadine rushed out to the garage to meet them. The bodyguard opened the trunk and she emerged, none the worse for wear. Nadine thanked and dismissed the bodyguard

"Come in the house and I'll fix you a drink. Maybe it will help you relax after this horrible ordeal." Yuke nodded.

As they walked to the den, Nadine informed Yuke that Marcus would be out of town until Tuesday afternoon, Yuke smiled, lightly pursed her lips, and blew Nadine a kiss.

"You can stay here until then if you wish," doing an air kiss back.

"I'll need more clothes and my make-up," she said softly.

"I can take care of that honey, don't worry," Nadine replied.

"I left some lights on, so the police and others would think I'm still home."

"Good idea, my dear."

The evening wore on and the two women consumed a fair amount of alcohol.

Yuke was laying with her head in Nadine's lap when she looked up and asked, "What is the secret project you call "Green Light" all about?"

"Oh… so you thought you could get me drunk, and I would spill the beans, huh?" Nadine said laughing.

Yuke smiled, "No, I thought if we were killing our husbands over it, I should have some idea what it is, don't you think?"

"Come-on sweetie, we've had too much to drink to talk about that stuff now, I'll tell you in the morning, I promise." They stood and walked hand in hand to Nadine's bedroom, closed the double doors, and turned off the light.

The next morning Nadine went into work to check on a few items that had been on her to-do list. An hour later she came home and found Yuke in the kitchen wearing one of her bathrobes and eating breakfast that the hired cook had made for her.

"You okay?" Nadine asked.

"Sure – just need a shower and a change of clothes."

"I have some time this morning, so when you are ready we can discuss the business we didn't get to last night. Oh, help yourself to anything in the closet or make-up table."

Thirty minutes later they met in the library. Nadine shut the double doors and closed the blinds. They each sat in a comfortable leather easy chair across from each other.

"This information in itself will make us millionaires many times over. The weapon has been completed and tested and retested several times. It performed flawlessly every time. We purchased three farm animals for the test – a pig, a goat, and a cow. The government has no knowledge or inkling of its existence."

"How does it work and to what purpose?" Yuke asked, leaning closer to hear Nadine's answer.

"We call it *Green Light*, because it involves a Green Laser. Of all the laser light colors, green is the most powerful. It's a hand held weapon that weighs 2.5 pounds. If you include the high-power scope that brings the weight to 3.5 pounds. The length is 32 inches. Its primary use is to kill a person at long range. However, the person won't die right away, but they most certainly will die within 48 hours without a trace of evidence of what caused their death."

Yuke's eyes were wide and her expression was of wild curiosity. "Tell me more," she blurted out.

"It's untraceable because there isn't any wound. We have tested it up to two miles from shooter to target. The concentrated spores allow 1,000 hits before reloading is necessary. We developed a new extremely powerful battery as the power source. Before we developed this one, the old battery was the size of a golf cart. Now our battery is the size of a nine volt with three times the power."

"What does the target die of?" she wanted to know.

"Anthrax."

"Anthrax?" Yuke shouted.

"Yes… the anthrax spores are in a micro-fine dust form that are placed in an aerosol container in a green laser beam and pointed at the target. When the trigger is pulled there isn't any sound. But when the laser blast with the Anthrax hits the victim's bare skin, the anthrax does its business of absorbing into the skin within a micro-second,. The victim will perish within 48 hours without a mark on his or her body. Primarily, the weapon would be used for an assassination of a VIP or head of state. However, I'm sure the people that purchase the plans to build it will come up with many more sadistic ways to use it. That's the basic use and function of our weapon."

She couldn't believe what she had just heard.

"Oh my God." Yuke's eyes and mouth were wide open as she put her hands to her face.

"I can see that there would be a huge demand for this kind of weapon. You're right… it would bring in millions," Yuke said.

Nadine sat quietly to let her absorb the possibilities.

"Another of our secrets that will bring us millions

more is named "Abilene Gray," and it's almost complete. I would estimate we would make at least 300 million right out of the gate. With my husband out of the way, you can come live with me and help in the business until we are rich beyond our dreams"

"We will have to deal with General Chang and the Chinese government and that won't be easy," Yuke said.

"Don't worry your pretty little head about it. My friends at the CIA or FBI can assist us with that if needed. We can tell them the Chinese are watching us and have tried to hack into the company's computer. They'll take it from there. Our security team will be on special alert," Nadine assured her.

"How do you want me to kill your husband?" Yuke asked.

"I think his death should be with the same gun used to murder your husband. We'll have to lure him to a place and time suitable for him to die."

"Won't the police connect the bullets to both killings?" she asked.

"I don't care if they do. I obtained the gun from a Seattle gang member, by way of one of my security team who disappeared shortly after he gave it to me. It's a Rugger 22 semi-automatic short barrel. It came with a homemade water bottle and steel wool silencer strapped onto the barrel."

"How did you get him to do that?" Yuke asked.

"Simple. I gave him a quick roll in the hay and he was mine," Nadine laughed and was thinking how easy it was to deal with men, because sex was their weakness.

12

Tuesday, 9:30 AM, Frank was in his office busily setting up the recordings while waiting for Marcus to arrive. Their appointment was scheduled for 10:00 AM. He made a fresh pot of coffee. Frank didn't quite understand why he felt so nervous. He looked out the window and saw the same two Feds sitting in their car across the street. They were looking at what appeared to be a map.

Damn, I hope Marcus is on time and those two clowns don't bother us during our meeting.

He moved away from the window.

Frank turned around as Marcus opened the door.

"Come in Mr. Radcliffe, please take this chair," Frank said, pointing to the one close to the computer. "Would you care for a fresh cup of coffee, sir?"

"Good morning Mr. Martini, and no thank you for your offer of coffee. I would like to get right down to business, if you don't mind."

Frank walked to the door and locked it, flipping the open sign to closed, then dropped the blinds and closed them. Back at his desk he reached over and unplugged his landline.

"I want you to be able to hear every word and see the video as clearly as possible," Frank said as he slipped the disk into his computer.

After the disk had finished Marcus Radcliffe sat back in his chair with a stunned expression. His face had grown pale and he looked as though he was in a state of shock.

"Oh my God... I didn't think she wanted me dead. Greed has overtaken her senses. Our love life has all but stopped over the last year. That's why I thought she was having an affair. I'm not bothered about her infidelity that much, but with another woman is surprising." he finally said.

"There is one other thing that I observed and it was not recorded. It took place in the lobby of the hotel."

"What was that?" Radcliffe asked.

"A man met with your wife and had her sign a document. By the sight of him he appeared to be employed by the government."

"Oh, yes, I sent him there to contact her. We had been awarded a new government contract. He first brought it here for our signatures. I signed it and sent him to see her for her signature."

"Okay, that explains that guy. Any instructions on what to do now, sir?"

"Shouldn't we go to the police with this information

and have the two of them arrested?"

"I'm afraid I can't do that yet"

"Why not?" Marcus wanted to know.

"Well the information I acquired by bugging their rooms and phone was obtained by illegal means. Therefor an attorney wouldn't be able to have it admitted into evidence. I could end up in a pile of trouble. We need to get solid evidence against them before we get the police involved."

"Okay – how do we accomplish that?" Marcus wanted to know.

"Just keep working the case until they make a mistake."

"Did you get anything from her phone that would help?"

"No, not anything more than we already know."

"Nadine is expecting me home this afternoon, so she will most likely be at the office about now. I need to go home to retrieve our secret diagrams and plans of the *Green Light and Abilene Gray* data. They are each stored in a secret room in our home."

"My friend Tommy Saliman and I will accompany you and provide for your safety. Does that meet with your approval?"

"Yes, I believe it would be a good idea," Mr. Radcliffe answered.

"I'll call him now." Frank dialed Tommy's number.

"Frankie boy, what can I do for ya?"

Frank explained the situation.

"See ya in fifteen," Tommy said and hung up.

Frank didn't try to explain to Marcus that Tommy was still on the job with Seattle's P.D. Frank thought that may be a concern for Marcus.

Tommy arrived right on time, his big frame stood in Frank's office doorway.

"He'll do," Marcus said, marveled by Tommy's size.

They all traveled in Marcus's car. When they arrived, Marcus pushed a button on a remote and the gate opened. As they passed through, a security guard waived. The windows of the car had a dark tint to them; the guard couldn't see inside.

Mr. Radcliffe stopped the car at the entrance to his home, and they all walked to the front door. Mr. Radcliffe punched in the security code, the massive front doors were unlocked, and the alarm and cameras were disarmed. The three men entered and walked to the library.

"Gentlemen, please wait here and watch for anyone who may be in the house," Marcus said. He walked over to a certain section of the bookshelf and pressed a book inward. An undetectable door opened and Marcus disappeared within. Minutes later a Chinese lady walked past. She saw the men standing there and assumed they were Nadine's security detail. Frank recognized her as Nadine's lover, Yuke. She continued on her way to wherever she was going. Marcus reappeared carrying a three ring binder with computer disks in plastic sleeves. He looked flushed and was sweating.

"Mr. Martini can I use your computer to work on these disks and make a few changes that will cause this program to malfunction? Then I will bring them back and put them where they were in the secret room. Nadine won't be any the wiser."

The three men returned to the car and headed for Frank's office. The same two Feds were still sitting in their car outside Frank's office building. *What the hell did they want? Maybe he would go out later and approach them.*

Marcus hurriedly put the first of the disks in Frank's computer, opened it and made a copy. He continued until all the disks were copied. Frank was peering over Marcus's shoulder, seeing the objects on the screen. They were completely foreign to him. To Frank it looked as though it may be some sort of genetic code, with strange signs and odd numbers. Marcus copied all the disks. Then started over with the originals, making changes as he worked. Marcus was deleting things and adding others. He continuing until he was satisfied each disk had been compromised.

When they arrived back at the Radcliffe's home, Marcus put everything back in its place. He felt that if his wife tried to sell the weapons information to anyone, it would not work. In fact it would kill the person that tried to use the weapon. Whoever her buyers were, they would most likely kill her and her accomplice on the spot.

They each went back to Frank's office.

Frank slipped Tommy a hundred and said, "Thanks, Tommy for your help on such short notice."

"Not a problem Frankie boy. Glad to help," he turned and shook Marcus's hand and left.

"Now, Mr. Radcliffe, I must keep you alive and safe. Do you remember the Chinese lady you saw on the information I showed you this morning? I saw her at your house while we were there the first time. She walked past while Tommy and I were waiting in the library."

"Do you think I should call Nadine and let her know I'm in town?"

"That is up to you sir. You know the lady that is supposed to kill you is probably at your house as we speak." Frank looked out the window again and frowned.

Those two Feds were well trained; someone up the line told them to sit and they are obeying their master obediently.

13

Marcus thought perhaps he should go to a small motel, book in under a phony name, and pay cash. A large tip usually allows one to do that sort of thing and avoid showing proof of identification.

"Frank, I'm sure Nadine will send our security team to look for me – maybe I should go to Bremerton, Washington. I have a friend there who lives on his yacht. I'm sure he would let me stay there for a few days," Marcus said.

"I like that plan. Remember, don't use your credit cards or your phone for anything," Frank stressed.

"I don't have much cash on me. I'll need clothing and other things," Marcus said.

"You need to visit your bank and withdraw a large amount of cash. You'll need it to tide you over. Then buy a burner phone. Use it to call me only and don't give the number to anyone until you are safe and this mess is over."

"The last place they will have been able to trace you

is from your bank. If they connect you to me somehow, you know I won't give you up."

Marcus shook Frank's hand. "Thank you for the help," Marcus said squeezing Frank's hand firmly, then turned and was walking away when Frank reminded him to stay in touch.

Frank needed to pay a visit to the Feds that were waiting outside. He walked down the back stairs of his building to the parking lot. There was twenty feet between his building and the one next door. He ducked down to lessen his image and ran across the empty space until he was in back of the next building. He continued to walk to the other end of that building and then turned the corner, walked to the street, approached their car from behind. Frank could see the one in the passenger seat was reading a paper and the other was looking up at Frank's office window. Frank approached from the passenger side. The window was rolled down and Frank shouted, "What the hell do you guys want with me?" The man in the passenger seat jerked and crumpled his newspaper. Frank thought maybe the guy pissed his pants, too. The other guy for some reason leaned on the horn, like it would serve as some sort of protection.

The man in the passenger seat finally said, "We wanted to talk with you when you were alone."

"Who are you, and who sent you?" Frank asked angrily.

The driver slipped his hand inside his suit jacket pocket. Frank already had his gun out and pointed at the man.

"Remove your hand very slowly or you're both dead." The driver did as Frank asked. With his credentials in hand, he handed them over to the man in the passenger seat who passed them on to Frank. Frank flipped them open and read the initials – FBI. He lowered his weapon and said, "So, I'll ask you for the second time. What the hell do you want with me?"

"Hop in the back... we'll explain," the driver said.

Frank opened the rear door and slid in among the trash that had collected there.

"We've been watching you ever since you visited the La Vista Carmel. Let's just say, we like to keep our eye on people who are in contact with our vendors, like the Radcliffe's. They are important people to us. It's our job to watch over them," the driver said while staring straight ahead.

"I assure you my dealings with Marcus Radcliffe are not in any way harmful to their business, to them, or, for that matter, to our country!" Martini shouted.

"Where is Mister Radcliffe now?" The man in the passenger seat asked.

"When he left my office, he told me he had business to take care of. I really don't know where he was going. Perhaps you should contact his wife. She may have some idea."

"Might be a good idea. Does she know about you?" he asked.

"No, I doubt it, and I would just as soon keep it that way," Frank said.

"If you hear from Radcliffe, contact us right away." the driver said. Frank smiled and flipped them off as he got out of the rear car seat. As he walked back to his office Frank couldn't help wondering if the Feds had bugged his phone or his apartment. Frank did an electronic sweep of his car, phone, office, and apartment. Not finding anything he was relieved, but he knew they could plant them at any time. He would make it a point to do a sweep every week, until this case had ran its course.

Marcus contacted his friend, Ben Swanson, the owner of the yacht he would be staying on for the next few days. He used his new burner phone as Frank had asked. It felt strange in his hand, as it was much smaller and didn't contain all the bells and whistles of his regular phone. No GPS. Ben gave Marcus explicit instructions on how to reach his yacht club.

"I can see the parking area from my galley window. I'll be looking for you. I'll have to open the electronic card gate to let you in. Club members who rent slips are the only ones allowed to have a key card," Ben said.

Nadine glanced at her cell phone – no messages – and it was well past the time for Marcus to be home. She dialed his number and waited. It went to message, but she didn't leave one.

That's not like him; he's always very dependable and prompt. She dialed another number.

"Max Neal," a voice said. Max was in charge of the Radcliffe's security team.

"Good evening Max, I'm getting a little concerned about Marcus," her voice was steady and strong.

"He was due to arrive home over four hours ago and I haven't heard from him. I've tried calling him with no success. Is there any way you can locate him?"

"Don't worry. We'll find him, and I'll get back with any update," Max replied.

Max opened a drawer in his desk and pulled out a small handheld black box and pushed a button; a red LED light came on. He walked over to a computer screen and watched a red dot moving close to Bremerton, Washington.

Unknown to the Radcliffe's, Max had placed a tracking device on each of their cars for their security. An hour later the dot stopped moving. Max zoomed in on the location. The map revealed it was the Bremerton Eagle Yacht Club. He called Nadine and told her what he had found.

"Do you want me to go check on him?" Max asked.

"No, that isn't necessary Max, I know who he is

visiting, and I'm sure he is alright. Thank you for your work," Nadine clicked off. She stood in the dining room with Yuke. "How in hell did he find him so quickly?"

"Maybe your security team has you bugged."

"Maybe," Nadine said.

"Does that yacht club have any significance to you?"

"Only a little. I've never been there but Marcus has an old friend that lives on his yacht in Bremerton. I wonder why he would go there without letting me know."

The house phone rang.

"Maybe that's him," Nadine said while picking up.

"Hello, Radcliffe residence," she said.

"May I speak to Mrs. Radcliffe?" the person asked.

"Speaking," she said.

"Mrs. Radcliffe, this is agent Paul Remington of the FBI."

"How may I help you, Mr. Remington?"

"I would like to know if you have heard of a private investigator by the name of Frank Martini that lives and works here in Seattle."

"No, I don't believe I have met such a person. Why are you asking?"

"Periodically, we keep tract of our vendors, and Mr. Martini's name came up during a check as being in contact with Mr. Radcliffe."

"Mr. Radcliffe isn't here at the moment, but when I see him I'll ask him. May I ask for your number so he can return the call?" Agent Remington recited his number.

"Please have him call me after you give him my message, and thank you for the help ma'am, Good bye."

"Yuke, it sounds like we may have a new player in the game. Tomorrow I want you to find out about a private investigator whose business is here in Seattle by the name of Frank Martini. Have you ever heard that name before?"

"No, it's not a familiar name to me," she responded.

"No one knows you're here, so you can use one of our cars and pay him a visit."

Yuke typed in Seattle, WA, investigators on her phone and Frank Martini's name and business address popped up. No residential address was listed.

"You don't have to contact him personally, but if you can take his picture and find out where he lives it would help. You should probably wear a disguise. You don't want General Chang to find out you are out and about."

14

Marcus pulled into the yacht club's parking lot. He emerged from his car carrying a large traveling bag. Marcus walked toward the gangway that lead to the electronic gate. He could see the ramp was at a steep decline, because it was low tide. Ben had already started up the ramp waving and shouting "Hello." Marcus smiled and waved back.

"How are you old friend?" Marcus said cheerily.

"It's so good to see you," Ben replied.

When they reached the bottom of the ramp Ben said, "Down this way to E dock. I'm the third slip on the left." As they stepped aboard Ben's yacht, Marcus noticed an overweight brown shorthaired Dachshund there to greet them.

"Marcus, I want you to meet my first mate, Hudson. Take your time getting to know him. He is friendly as long as you don't make any sudden moves toward me – at that point he'll bite. While the weather remains warm he sleeps outside on the deck with his special pillow."

"Marcus reached down and patted Hudson on the

head, "I'll keep that in mind, Hudson." Hudson's tail was waging so hard you would have thought it was going to fly off.

"Let me take your bag. I'll show you to your quarters. Then we'll have a drink and you can bring me up to date on what's happening in your life."

The two men drank and talked far into the night before retiring. Ben was up first the next morning hovering over the galley stove. Marcus appeared minutes later with arms stretched over his head and yawning. Hudson was at Ben's feet looking for scraps.

"How did you sleep?" Ben asked.

"It was the best night sleep I've had in years. I felt like I was sleeping on a cloud." Marcus looked outside at the early morning sunrise and calm water.

"Ben, you certainly picked a beautiful spot to live."

"After breakfast, I'll take you on a tour of the city, and later we will go out on the water and have lunch. Oh, how do you like your eggs, Marcus?"

"Over medium – let me give you a hand," Marcus said.

"Not a chance, old buddy. You're my guest."

The two men ate and continued talking. Marcus finally decided to tell Ben what Frank Martini had discovered. When he finished, Ben was sitting back in his chair with his jaw open.

"You have to be kidding. Please tell me this is a big joke."

"I'm afraid not, my friend."

"So, in effect you are hiding out."

"Yes, that's exactly what I'm doing. No one has the slightest idea where I am."

"My God man, what in hell do you plan to do?"

"Stay put for a couple of days, if you don't mind."

"You know you are welcome here for as long as necessary," Ben said.

"Thanks Ben. Perhaps we should discuss more pleasant things."

They cleaned up the dishes and left for the city.

———

Yuke was in the back parking lot of Frank's office building. She dialed Frank's number. A recording started and she hung up. She waited an hour without any sign of Frank and returned to Nadine's home. The sky was cloudy with rumbles of thunder. The wind had picked up and the air was heavy with humidity. A storm was on its way and appeared imminent.

"Damn rain," she said in a low whisper.

Nadine was on her computer in an attempt to find pictures of the Bremerton Eagle Yacht Club when Yuke buzzed her to open the gate. She parked the car in the garage just as the rain began.

"No luck," She said.

"Don't worry sweetie, I'll have Max send one of his men to get a picture of this mysterious private investigator."

After talking to Mrs. Radcliffe, the two FBI agents left their assigned post in front of Frank's office and reported back to headquarters.

The next day Max sent a man who took several pictures of men coming and going from Frank's building. He stayed there until mid-afternoon. When he arrived back and reported to Max, they downloaded the pictures and brought them to Mrs. Radcliffe. Max, Yuke, and Nadine took their time viewing each of the photographs.

"There's nothing on any of the social websites under Frank Martini. I had one of my contacts run him on NCIC and found that this Martini guy is a retired police officer from the Seattle police department. No known wife or kids and no law suits in the past or active at this time." Max said.

"Yuke, do any of these pictures look familiar to you?" Nadine asked.

"No, no one at all. Wait minute... isn't this guy part of your security team?" she responded.

"No," Max said.

"I swear I saw him and another big guy in your house a few days ago."

Nadine bent down close to the pictures and pointed to the same one, "I've seen this man somewhere before. He looks vaguely familiar, like someone I have come across recently, but I can't put a name to him."

"Okay, I'll call Martini's office and make an

appointment with the pretext of needing his services. I'll use my pinhole camera to get a better shot. Maybe that will help" Max said.

Later that afternoon Max contacted Nadine and explained that he had a better close-up picture of Frank Martini and he would bring it to her.

"Yes, I remember seeing him at the Carmel hotel in California where we had our seminar last weekend. I'm sure of it. He was cozy with a couple of our members."

Ben and Marcus returned from the city tour and readied the boat for another tour, this time it would be around the Kitsap peninsula and Puget Sound. The homes built along the shore on both sides were spectacular. Most were nestled among the trees and vegetation. Ben was cruising at a slow speed and offering information along the way. They passed hundreds of inlets.

It would be easy for a stranger to get lost.

"Marcus, would you look in the drawer beside you? There is a paper menu in there for a place called, Do Stop By. It's a restaurant where you can call ahead for an order. They have a channel where you can bring your boat. They will deliver your order, kind of a waterway drive-thru." Ben was familiar with the menu and suggested the baked Albacore on a bed of lettuce with a honey walnut drizzle and slices of fresh avocado on the side.

"If it's what you are having, I'll have the same," Marcus said.

Ben called the order in, and by the time they got to the restaurant dock, it was waiting for them.

"I have a favorite cove where we can anchor and enjoy our lunch, along with a fine bottle of wine."

"You know Ben, I hadn't realized how long it's been since I've taken time to relax. God, I'm really enjoying this." The two men took their time and ate and drank.

"Sorry to tell you my friend, but it looks as though we are in for a storm. Look to the right – those dark clouds are heavy with rain. I'm going to head back to the slip."

"It's something all of us who live in the Pacific Northwest learn to accept," Marcus answered. Their journey back to the yacht club was at full throttle. They had just pulled under the metal cover and in the slip when the rain hit. They each laughed. Ben suggested a game of cribbage, at five dollars a point.

"Break out the board. I'll keep score," Marcus smiled and patted Ben on the back.

15

Nadine handed her the loaded gun she used to kill Yuke's husband, along with the information where Marcus was staying with his friend, Ben Swanson. She warned Yuke that a private yacht club no doubt had some sort of security, or else it wouldn't be called private.

"Somehow Marcus has figured out what our plans are. You'll need to find him,and kill him before he moves to another location, or tells anyone else, beside this Martini guy." She nodded and placed the revolver and silencer in her large purse, being careful to conceal it under an assortment of other items.

"I'll deal with Martini later," Nadine said.

Nadine called Max and told him to let her know if her husband's location changed. He assured her he would.

———

Frank's phone buzzed, the display showed it was Tommy.

"What's up Tommy?"

"I just wanted to let you know I'll be a free man in four days. I hope I can start working for you then," He said with a smile in his voice.

"Did you get your PI license like I told you?"

"Yup, sure did. I pulled a few strings and got it taken care of faster than normal."

"Your timing is great. I think we will be getting busy about then."

"Will it be on the same case I helped you with the other day?"

"Same one, but no names. You never know who may be listening," Frank said.

"Okay, buddy-boy see ya next week," Tommy hung up.

Tommy sat back in his chair, put his feet on the desk, and folded his hands in back of his head. Four more days, he said to himself. Four more days...

Marcus picked up his new cell phone and dialed Frank's number. Frank's display didn't show who was calling, it merely showed, 'Unregistered Caller.' Frank usually didn't bother with those kinds of calls, but something told him to answer this one.

"Hello, this is Frank. Who is calling?"

"Mr. Martini, it's Marcus Radcliffe. I wanted to check in with you."

"Oh, I'm sorry sir. The phone display only showed unregistered caller. It's good to hear from you. Have you settled in okay?"

"Yes, quite well, and I have to tell you, I'm thoroughly enjoying myself."

"I'm glad to hear that. It's good you called because I need to ask you a question. Do you know anyone named Max Smith?"

"No, the only man I know named Max, is Max Neal who's head of my security."

"Describe him."

"Well, he's about six foot, two hundred with black wavy hair. He wears an earring in his left ear."

"That's the same guy who visited me yesterday. I think your wife has connected the dots between you and I. Max, no doubt, has my picture and will show it to your wife. I'm positive she will remember seeing me at her conference in Carmel."

"What should we do, Frank?"

That was the first time Radcliffe has called me by my first name. It sounds to me we're now on a first name basis.

"I'm not sure if they know where you are. I think you need to be very careful and start thinking of some other places you can hide."

"I don't see how they could possibly know my location," Marcus answered.

"Well, if I were head of your security I would have a tracker somewhere on your car.

It might serve you well to check the underside of your vehicle. There may be a magnetic device there. If you find one, stomp on it hard then throw it in the water. And – let me know."

"Thanks Frank, will check it out right away," Marcus clicked off.

Marcus told Ben the conversation he had with Frank. The two men walked to the parking lot and with each of them taking a side of Marcus's car, they got down on their backs and searched the underside of the car. Ben found the device and pulled it off. It was a small, square black box with an even smaller antenna. A red LED light was blinking on and off. Ben gave it to Marcus who put it on the ground and gave it a hard stomp. On their way back to the boat, Marcus threw what was left of it as far as he could out into the water. The red LED red light blinked once and went out, as it sank to the bottom.

Marcus called Frank immediately and told him of their find and how he disposed of the device.

"Good, maybe they haven't tracked you yet, but I wouldn't count on it. You should be planning your next move soon."

"I will Frank, I'll leave in the morning and let you know when I get to wherever I end up." They hung up.

16

Yuke packed dark clothing, a black wet suit, and a pair of sneakers that belonged to Nadine. She had checked the distance between Seattle and Bremerton on her cell phone. It showed 65 miles and a one hour and thirty minutes of drive time. She waited until eleven in the evening before she started for Bremerton, WA. She wanted to catch Marcus off guard, hoping he would be in a sound sleep.

An hour and a half later, she pulled into the yacht club parking lot and parked next to the club office building. There were a couple nightlights burning outside giving her just enough of a glow to see where she was going. She spotted a signboard listing the names and locations of each club member's slip. She used the small flashlight that she put in a pocket of the wet suit to read the sign. She scrolled down the list until she saw Ben Swanson... E3L, which translated to E dock third slip on the left. Yuke went back to her car and changed into the wet suit and sneakers, left her car keys on top of the driver's side front tire. There wasn't any movement or sound coming from the dock area. It was dark except for a few scattered low-wattage lights.

The water was at low tide and she walked to the edge carrying a waterproof bag with the gun and silencer inside. She waded waist deep into the cold water. The wet suit covered her body except for her hands, ankles, and face. She swam out and around the fence barrier then doubled back to the dock on the other side of the security gate. The dock had a ladder on the end. Yuke climbed up and stood quietly, observing her surroundings. She took the gun out of the bag and attached the silencer, then found E dock. *Third on the left* she said to herself. She bent as low to the dock as she could, trying to create a smaller profile. Gun in her right hand, she stepped aboard and continued toward the main cabin. Hudson growled. She stopped and turned toward the sound. He charged and jumped at her clamping his teeth around her right wrist causing great pain. She jerked against him and the gun went off. The bullet penetrated the glass window in the cabin and lodged in the side of the refrigerator. She was screaming in pain and slinging Hudson's body around trying to get him to release his clinched jaws. She released her grip on the gun, and it hit the deck and slid into the water. Yuke lost her footing and also fell in the water. Hudson let go of her and was trying to find a place he could get out of the water. She swam back toward shore with painful difficulty.

The noise had awoken Ben and Marcus. Ben turned on the cabin light and saw the shattered glass.

"Marcus, don't come in here without your shoes. There's glass all over the floor."

Ben called for Hudson, there wasn't any response. He got his flashlight and went out on deck. There was blood near Hudson's bed-pillow. Ben called out for Hudson again and again. Soon a few lights came on in other boats. They were wondering what all the noise was about.

She reached shore and ran to her car, fumbling for the keys, then she got in without taking time to dry off, she sped away with her wrist still bleeding and starting to swell.

Hudson finally made it to shore and started barking. "I'll go get him – he's probably pretty shook-up, Ben said. Marcus found a broom and had swept up the broken glass.

Ben returned with Hudson in his arms.

"He's alright," Ben said.

"I found something else," Marcus said, while pointing to the side of the refrigerator.

"Is that a bullet lodged in there?"

"Sure is… I need to call the police," Ben said.

Fifteen minutes later two officers arrived. Ben had gone up to the card gate to let them in. When they got to the boat, one of them began taking pictures. The other one asked Ben to give him an account of what had happened.

"I guess you could say my dog here saved our lives."

The other officer had taken a sample of the blood that was on the deck and placed it in an evidence bag. One officer left the boat and started interviewing other boat owners who had appeared on the dock.

"Were either of you hit or hurt?" The officer asked.

"No sir, just shaken up," Ben replied while holding Hudson in his arms.

"Then the blood had to be from the person that fired the shot."

"When I heard a scream, it sounded like it was a woman, and the funny thing is neither of us heard a gunshot." Ben said.

"Do either of you know why anyone would be trying to shoot you?"

"Absolutely not," Ben responded. The officer tweaked his face as if he was not sure Ben was telling the truth.

"A detective will contact you later in the morning. Don't disturb anything until he gets here."

The other cop came back and said, "No one heard or saw anyone." The officers bid Ben and Marcus a good night, handed them their business cards, and left. Ben locked both doors to the salon. He had never had to take any kind of precaution in the past, and it bothered him to have to do it now. Ben walked back to his bedroom and laid Hudson on the bed.

"I'm going to let him stay with me the rest of the night."

She pulled to a stop in back of an office building, changed into her clothes then found an all-night drug store. She picked up a bottle of peroxide and a box of bandages. When she was back in her car she called Nadine who answered on the first ring. "Did everything go okay?" Nadine asked. Yuke told her what had taken place. Nadine was pacing back and forth with a worried look on her face. She was concerned about Yuke being caught.

"Oh, my God!" Are you going to be alright?"

"I'm alright for now but when I get back I'm sure I will need stitches on my right wrist. That damn dog was vicious. I didn't expect anything like that."

"Did anyone see you?"

"No, the whole thing happened so fast. The time I stepped aboard until I fell back into the water was less than a minute. Then everything was quiet."

"Where is the gun now?" Nadine asked.

"When I last saw it, the gun hit the deck and slid overboard into the water."

"Shit – we need to get it back before you leave Bremerton."

"How do you expect me to do that?" Yuke asked.

"Wait a couple of hours, go back to a spot near the yacht club, put the wet suit back on, quietly swim out to the boat, and dive for it. You already know which side of the boat where the gun fell into the water. I doubt if it is over ten feet deep there."

"The water will be completely dark," Yuke said.

"The flashlight that is in the wet suit is waterproof. Use it." Nadine answered.

Yuke really didn't want to go back there, but she knew Nadine was right – he had to retrieve that gun.

She changed back into the wet suit and sneakers. She drove to an area about a hundred yards from the yacht club and walked in the shadows until she reached the water's edge. She stopped and listened. All was quiet.

The water was calm and she walked out until she could swim breaststroke all the way to Ben's yacht. She silently went below the surface and to the bottom. The light beam was narrow but it showed the bottom to be of a sandy texture. She spotted the gun almost immediately and picked it up by the barrel. She swam away from the boats before coming to the surface and slowly made her way to shore. Still no sounds or lights. She worked her way back to her car. The salty water was burning her open wound and the only towel she had brought was still wet from her previous swim. Yuke changed back again into her street clothes and drove to the nearest motel and got a room. The clerk on duty was not happy being awakened at three thirty in the morning and did not hide his displeasure. Yuke went to her room, showered, and attended to her wrist.

It was then she discovered her anklet was missing. She was sure it must have come off during her fall into the water. She showered and cleaned the salt water off the wet suit. It wasn't easy bandaging her wound with only one hand. Once the wound was bandaged, she went to bed and was able to get a few hours' sleep and was back in Seattle by eleven the next morning.

Nadine met her at the door. "Oh, you poor dear. We need to get you to a doctor." I have a friend who practices out of his home. He only has a few select patients and is very discreet."

After the doctor examined her, he said, "I'll need to do a small amount of surgery right now." An hour later the surgery was complete. The doctor bandaged Yuke's wrist and gave her a bottle of antibiotics.

I'll need to see you every day for the next two weeks. I want to make sure there is no infection. Can you give me any information on the dog that bit you? There is always a chance of rabies and if that is the case, you have to go through a series of rabies' shots and those are very painful." Nadine paid the doctor and they left.

They headed for Nadine's house. Yuke went to bed as soon as she could. Nadine cleaned the gun, freeing it of the salt water residue. She knew that the salt water had penetrated the silencer and would have rusted the steel wool rendering it ineffective. She found a new empty water bottle, stuffed it with steel-wool, and clamped it back on the barrel. It was ready for the next time she would need it.

17

Marcus was up early and had finished packing his gear. He offered to pay Ben for the damages to the yacht. Ben refused and told Marcus he was welcome to stay or come back to visit anytime. Hudson was wagging his tail as if to say goodbye. Marcus bent down and patted him on the head. "Thanks, buddy for saving our butts last night." Ben shook Marcus's hand and Marcus left.

Marcus wondered if the woman who was on the boat last night was Nadine or the Chinese woman she was having an affair with. His new cell phone ring broke the silence. He only knew of one person who had its number.

"Hey Frank, how are things going on your end?" Frank could tell that something was wrong by the unsteadiness in Marcus's voice.

"Nothing new here, but somehow I feel you're about to tell me something."

"You are a very perceptive person my friend." Marcus answered.

"Are you okay?"

"Yes, but I need to bring you up to date," Marcus said. He told Frank what happened the night before.

"My God, man… that was a close call. They must have already tracked you to the yacht club before you destroyed the tracking device. That would be my guess."

"It appears that way," Marcus responded.

"Are you still there at the yacht club?" Frank asked.

"No, I left Ben's yacht about thirty minutes ago. I'm not sure where I'll end up next, but when I get there I'll give you a call."

"Marcus, wherever you go keep checking to make sure you're not being followed.

I want you to know, I've made copies of all the information I showed you about Nadine and the Chinese woman including their conversations. I will take the copies and your original disks of your secret project plans to my safe deposit box. I don't feel they are secure in my safe at my apartment."

"I agree – that's a good move."

"Let me hear from you when you can," Frank said and clicked off.

Nadine was at home trying to assess the whole situation… *If Marcus is hiding, he no doubt knows we have tried to kill him. Why hasn't he gone to the police to have us arrested? The private investigator he hired was at our conference in Carmel. So, he must have given Marcus details of Yuke and me. We did discuss our plan of killing each other's husbands. I need to contact our attorney.*

"Hello, this is Nadine Radcliffe. Is Rodney in?"

"Yes, Mrs. Radcliffe, I'll connect you."

Rodney Ashland had been the Radcliffe's attorney for the past ten years.

"Good afternoon Nadine, how have you and Marcus been? It seems like forever since we've talked," he said.

"We're fine, Rodney. If you don't mind, I have a legal question for you. Perhaps you can answer it over the phone."

"I'll give it a try." he replied.

"I know you're aware that a good deal of our company business is with our government. Well, I think someone may have recorded one of my conversations without my knowledge. What I need to know is would that recording be admissible in court, if it was recorded without my knowledge?"

"A quick answer is definitely not. In most cases it violates Federal and State wiretapping statutes. Does that help?" Rodney asked.

"Oh yes, my dear man, it surely does, and thank you so much."

"You're welcome and give my best to Marcus," Rodney said and hung up.

So, that's the reason poor old Marcus hasn't called the cops. He can't prove anything.

When the police ran the ballistics on the bullet recovered from the yacht's refrigerator, it matched a gun used in a homicide a year ago in Portland, Oregon. Other than the distorted bullet and a thin gold anklet chain with a Chinese charm on it, the Bremerton, Washington police didn't have any other leads to go on. The police had checked with the local hospitals for dog bite wounds the day after the incident was reported,. That was also a dead end. The Chinese charm on the anklet turned out to be a popular good luck charm sold by the millions.

Frank Martini called the Bremerton PD and asked for the officers who had handled the original call in the early morning from the yacht club. He spoke with a female who handled all of the incoming calls. The woman looked up the case and told Frank the officers were not available, but she could have them call him back. Frank gave her his cell number. Two hours later, Frank spoke with one of the two officers. He found out the case was turned over to detective, John Delton. Frank told the officer about his background as a retired Seattle police officer and his current private investigation service. He was hoping for a little professional courtesy.

"I'll see if I can transfer you to his extension," the officer said.

"John Delton," a booming voice said.

"Hey John, this is Frank Martini, retired PD from Seattle.

"What can I do for you, Frank?"

"I understand you were given a case that took place on a yacht at the Bremerton Eagle Yacht Club a couple of days ago."

"Yeah, we don't have much to go on," John said.

"My friend, Marcus Radcliffe, was one of the people on the yacht when it happened. Would it be possible to bring me up to date on the case file?"

"What was your rank and badge number when you retired?"

"Sargent, badge number 105 and ID SW22137.

John clicked away on his computer, verifying Frank's information.

"Sorry for the delay Frank... just needed to check."

"I understand, John."

"The only two pieces of evidence we have is the remains of a single 22 cal. bullet I pulled from the yacht's refrigerator and a small gold anklet chain with a Chinese charm on it. I have nothing else to go on. Sorry."

"You sure it was a Chinese charm?"

"Yeah, we checked it out at a Chinese gift shop, and it was in the shape of a small dragon. They told us it was a good luck charm."

"Thanks John, I appreciate your help." They clicked off. Frank knew immediately the chain belonged to

Yuke. He decided to review the disk he recorded at the hotel between Nadine and Yuke when they were together in Yuke's room. He remembered Nadine giving her a massage. A few minutes into the recording he saw her lying face down on the bed and Nadine applying oil to her back. You could see she was wearing a gold anklet chain, but there wasn't a charm visible.

Frank hadn't talked to Marcus since yesterday. He wanted to tell Marcus the additional information he had uncovered.

"Hello Marcus. Where are you now?" he asked.

"I'm in Tacoma, staying at a Bed and Breakfast" Marcus answered.

"I have a small amount of news for you. I contacted John Edenton, a detective at Bremerton PD, who told me they recovered a gold anklet chain with a Chinese charm attached. I'm pretty sure Nadine's friend, Yuke Jun, was the person who was there trying to kill you."

18

Nadine and Yuke were having a quiet dinner alone in the dining room. Nadine had broiled two nice portions of salmon and prepared a green salad with baby shrimp. They sat in silence through most of the meal.

Nadine looked up and said, "Now that you are aware of what we have to offer as a new secret weapon, you should be thinking about how and whom you can approach for a first meeting." Nadine said.

"I've been a bit busy." Yuke replied.

"I have to deal with the FBI. They're going to want to know where I was at the time of my husband's death, or if I can help them with any other information."

"Just the same, you're in the spy business, and you know other people in that line of work. Maybe you've come in contact with someone who knows someone."

Yuke felt Nadine was pushing her and ignoring the more pressing issues that faced them. Nadine could tell that something was bothering Yuke by the expression on her face.

"What will you tell them when they question you?" Nadine asked.

"The truth of course."

"The truth? You haven't even told me what you did after we left each other that evening."

"I knew the police would notify me when they found him, and I wanted to be ready for them."

"Right after you and I parted, I went over to some friend's home. We drank wine and talked until late in the evening. Remember, you called my cell phone to let me know the job was done. I called my home and left a message for my husband to let him know where I was, and that I would be late. My friends decided I was too impaired to drive, so I spent the night at their place. I believe I have established a great alibi, don't you think?" Yuke said.

"I'm proud of you, my dear, you've covered your tracks nicely," Nadine replied.

"What about you?" Yuke asked.

"Oh, when I arrived home that night at 10:30, Marcus was already asleep. Marcus has a routine he follows each night. He brushes his teeth, drinks a warm toddy, then takes a mild sleeping aid. He's off to bed by 8:30. I went to our bedroom and set the clock back an hour, then I woke him up. I told him I wanted to have sex. He was ready in seconds. Ten minutes later he had finished. I made sure he noticed the time and my alibi was set," Nadine answered.

Both ladies looked at each other, laughed and hugged.

"Let's go to your place and you can get the things you need," Nadine suggested.

Nadine drove past Yuke's house to make sure no one was waiting at the front gate. Yuke was on the floor of the car in the back seat. Nadine circled around and approached the front gate. Yuke pushed the gate clicker and it opened. Next, she pushed the garage door opener, and Nadine drove into the garage. Yuke closed the door behind them. The two women entered the house, and Yuke could see everything was as she left it. The phone light was blinking; it showed ten messages were unanswered. She listened to each one. Seven were from the police wanting to talk with her, the rest were from General Chang.

"I think you should call the Seattle PD and invite them here to your home for the interview."

"Okay, but I won't talk to General Chang! If he ever got ahold of me, you would never see me again. I'm so afraid of that man. I've heard horrible stories of what he has done to people back in China," she answered.

"I understand. Pack a couple of suitcases with things you'll need, and I will take them back with me," Nadine said.

She went to her bedroom and began packing. This was the first time Nadine had ever been in Yuke's home. The decor was heavily Asian, and Nadine found it to be quite gaudy to her taste. She returned to the living room with two large pieces of luggage. They each took one and placed it in the trunk of Nadine's car.

"Yuke, you know it's been several days since your husband's death. You need to contact the morgue or the Chinese Consulate as to the disposition of his body."

"I already know the Chinese government will want the body shipped back to China, and they will expect me to travel with him."

"You had better take care of Marcus, so we can continue our plans," Nadine answered.

"Why don't you call Max and see if he knows where Marcus is hiding?"

Nadine dialed Max's number. "Do you have a location on Marcus?"

"I'm sorry I don't. He must have found the tracking device I had placed on his car,and removed it. Maybe you could check your credit card statement to see if he has used his card. See if he has purchased gas or lodging in the last couple days."

"Thanks Max, I will be in touch later," she said.

Nadine went to her computer and reviewed her online bank statements. There weren't any charges by Marcus at all. She found Marcus had made a one hundred thousand dollar withdrawal a few days ago.

It looks as though he's planning on staying away for a while. Marcus has to come back to work at some point, but he needs to feel safe. How can I entice him to come home?

Nadine wasn't sure what Marcus's private investigator had overheard between her and Yuke at the Carmel resort. She decided to blame Yuke for all of the problems with Marcus of late.

Nadine sat at her computer and typed out an email. It informed Marcus of her affair with the Chinese woman. She tried to tell him how sorry she was and how controlling Yuke had become. She accused her of killing her own husband, and how she was planning on killing him, so she could have me all to herself. Nadine went on to say she finally told Max about Yuke, and that Max said he would handle getting rid of her by telling the Chinese government where she was hiding. Nadine signed off and begged Marcus to come home. She pushed send. Marcus was on his computer and noticed an incoming email.

What a bunch of bullshit. She really must think I'm stupid enough to believe that crap.

He pushed the delete tab, and Nadine's email disappeared.

19

Yuke made the call to Detective Tyree of the Seattle PD.who had left the messages on her phone. The operator transferred her to his extension.

"Tyree," a strong male voice answered.

"Detective, this is Yuke Jun. I have been away, mourning the death of my husband. I see you have left several messages for me. How may I help you?"

"Mrs. Jun, I'm very sorry for your loss. I was wondering if you could come to my office for an interview. If you need transportation, I will send a car for you." His voice had changed to soft and soothing.

"I will help you in any way I can, but I would prefer that you come to my home, Detective. I would feel much more comfortable that way."

Yuke was sitting in her family room when the gate buzzer went off. She peered out the window and saw an unmarked car waiting at the gate. She pushed the gate opener and the unmarked police car started forward, stopping half way through the gate. A black limo had pulled up close to the police unit. Detective Tyree exited his car showing his badge. The limo backed up, turned, and drove away. Yuke knew the limo belonged to General Chang, and a chill came over her. Detective Tyree watched the limo until it was out of site. Tyree had brought FBI agent Ziggy Morris with him for the interview.

She hadn't been home for a few days and lacked anything to serve with the tea she had prepared for Tyree and agent Morris. Yuke greeted them at the front door and lead them to the dining room table. She didn't bother to ask if they wanted tea, she just poured it.

"Thank you Mrs. Jun." they each replied.

"Your welcome gentleman," she answered.

"First Mrs. Jun, we want to tell you we are very sorry for your loss.

She nodded and bowed her head slightly.

"Please gentleman you may call me Yuke."

"Alright Yuke, we would like to ask you if you know of anyone who would have any reason to kill your husband or why."

"No, no one."

"Had he received any death threats?"

"Not to my knowledge," she responded with tears beginning to form in her eyes.

"I'm sorry to have to ask you these questions, but so

far we don't have any leads in his murder. I know it's painful, however I have to ask you, "Where were you on the night of his demise?"

Yuke proceeded to tell them her alibi story. She even played the phone recording with the date and time, telling her husband she would be late coming home. She gave them her friend's names and phone number to substantiate her story.

Agent Morris asked if she would be willing to take a lie detector test.

"I'm sorry gentleman, but as a foreign national working for the Chinese Government I believe I have diplomatic protection. You will have to contact the Chinese counsel."

"I think that will be all for now. We will be in touch." Thank you Mrs. Jun for allowing us to speak with you. "Oh one last thing… who was in the car that tried to gain entrance when we started in your gate earlier?"

"I have no idea. Sorry."

They shook her hand and left her home.

"I noticed the limo had a Chinese plate on the back of the vehicle," Agent Morris said to Tyree.

"I know," Tyree responded. Both men had a questionable look on their face.

"Something isn't right.

I'll try to get authorization to dump her phones," agent Morris commented.

"I'll see about the lie detector thing," Tyree said.

She watched them leave her property and made sure no one else came in.

General Chang had already sent Wang Jun's body back to China. The General needed to speak with Yuke. He was sure she had information on weapons the Radcliffe Company was developing for the CIA or FBI. Chang was well aware of Yuke's involvement with Nadine Radcliffe, but he thought it was only for the purpose of spying on her.

She called Nadine on an untraceable cell phone.

"How did it go?" Nadine asked

"No problem at all, but now I need to get out of here, and I don't think the hiding in the trunk trick will work again. General Chang tried to enter the gate right behind the cops, but they prevented him or his goons from coming in. My best guess is they will make another attempt within 24 hours," Yuke replied.

"I want you to pack a medium size box with things you need and want to keep, like jewelry, pictures, bank accounts, clothes, cell-phone and other things of importance. Seal it closed and address it to my house. Call UPS for a pick up. Bill it to me, then place the package on the front porch and give them the gate code.

Next I want you to call a pizza shop for a delivery and give them a credit card number for payment. When he comes to the door, invite the kid in. Tell him you are in fear for your life. Offer him a large amount of money to help you sneak into his car without being seen. Tell him to bring you to my house and make sure your security alarm is on before you leave."

"Okay, I'll do it," Yuke said. She found a box and began filling it with various items. She put Nadine's address on the top along with her information as the sender and sealed it. The UPS office had told her the pick-up would be between 7 PM and 9 PM.

She put her gate and security remotes in her purse, and then she turned on all her interior lights, except the front entrance. She left all the exterior lights off. She wanted to keep the front entry as dark as possible while she was leaving and getting into the pizza delivery car.

She put on dark black clothing and a pair of black gloves with a black ski mask sitting on the table ready to go.

A few hours later the UPS had picked up the package at the front door. There wasn't any sign of General Chang.

When the pizza delivery arrived she hurried the delivery boy inside.

"Look young man, I'm in a world of hurt. I need your help badly," she said in a low shaky voice.

"What's wrong ma'am?" he said looking around like somebody was about to attack him.

"I'll pay you five hundred dollars if you will let me sneak into the back of your car before you leave here." The kid thought for a second. "Is this a joke? Are you kidding me? Am I on camera or something?"

"No, I'm dead serious," She answered with fear in her voice.

"Yeah, sure if you pay in cash and the cost of the pizza plus a tip."

"Deal," She said."

"What do I do with the pizza," the kid asked.

"Leave the damn thing on the table, and let's get the hell out of here."

Yuke put on her hat and gloves and crouched down beside the kid as they left the house and got into the car. Her heart was beating so fast she thought she was going to have a heart attack. Once they had cleared the gate and saw no one was following, she began to relax. She gave the kid seven hundred dollars. She told him if he ever told anyone about this she would have his balls cut off.

"Do you understand?" Yuke said as she reached around the seat and grabbed his crouch. The kid had already wet his pants. She knew he got the point. Nothing else was said during the remaining trip to Nadine's house.

20

Marcus was reading the local paper and sipping on a glass of Gentleman Jack Whiskey. He decided he needed a change of scenery for the evening. He asked the owner of the B&B where the nearest movie theater was located. A few minutes later he was on his way.

The red and blue lights appeared out of nowhere. They sped around him, clipping his front fender as they passed. Just that simple touch at an angle made Marcus' car go out of control, rolling over several times before coming to a stop on its side. The air bags deployed and pinned him to the seat with such force that he received a black eye and a bruised cheekbone. His right hand hit the rear view mirror and broke his thumb. The only other injuries he received were small cuts from the flying glass.

The police unit had spun around and hit a cement abutment. The officer crawled out and was lying on the ground next to his unit. He reached for his shoulder mic and called for help. His car lights were still flashing, red and blue, bouncing off the trees and the cement abutment. Another unit came to give assistance, and soon the paramedics arrived. One of the cops was directing traffic around the accident and another was putting up yellow crime scene tape. The news reporters were like a pack of hungry wolves. They were hollering with all sorts of questions. A news helicopter was circling above with its spotlight fixed on the two vehicles.

The paramedics had cut Marcus lose from his car, placed him on a hardboard, and strapped him down. They put a neck collar in place to prevent any additional injuries. They did the same for the cop. They were both placed into the ambulance and left code-three for St. Clare hospital. Marcus and the officer were both hooked up to an IV.

His cell phone was in his pants pocket and his restraints wouldn't allow him to reach for it. He knew he must get a hold of Frank as soon as possible.

The news people had already started gathering information on Marcus and the cop. The accident had made the early Chanel seven evening news, with sketchy information,. By nine o'clock the news had identified Marcus by name and showed a picture of his face, taken as he'd entered the hospital.

"Son of a bitch!" Marcus shouted. The nurse came running into his room.

"You must lay quiet," she said.

"I've got to get out of here," Marcus answered.

"We are keeping you overnight – you may have a concussion. You will probably be released in the morning."

"Where are my pants?"

"You can't go sir," she said.

"You don't understand… I need my cell phone."

"Oh – I'll get it for you."

She returned with his phone. He hurriedly called Frank.

"I'm on my way, and I'm bringing my friend Tommy," Frank hung up.

A short man entered Marcus' room and produced a badge.

"Mr. Radcliffe I need to ask you some questions," the man said.

"Okay," Marcus answered.

"The toxicology report showed you had a small amount of alcohol in your blood but not enough to be considered impaired. We have a statement from the officer that caused the accident. He admitted he was at fault."

"How about my car?" Marcus wanted to know.

"The county attorney will be in touch with you later. You'll need to contact your insurance company. Meanwhile your car was towed to a salvage lot. I'm not sure if it has any value left," the man said.

"Thanks for the information sir," Marcus answered.

Frank set his GPS for the hospitals address, and he and Tommy were on their way. Frank asked Tommy, "Are you carrying?"

"Always," Tommy answered.

"Sit back and relax – it's about an hour drive," Frank said.

21

Nadine had also heard the TV newscast about her husband's accident. She retrieved the gun and silencer from the secure hiding place and put it on the table. Nadine walked to Yuke's room and told her what had happened to Marcus and where he was. "I'll leave in a few minutes," Yuke said without hesitation. Nadine looked up the hospital's location and wrote it down for her.

"No doubt Marcus has contacted his friend, Mr. Martini. You'll need to be extremely careful." she nodded. Nadine handed her the car keys and kissed her goodbye.

Frank pulled into the hospitals parking area and found a place close to the main entrance. All was quiet as they walked into the hospital's large waiting room.

"Come on Tommy, we need to alert hospital security that there may be an attempt on Marcus' life." They each showed their IDs to the head of security and told him they were Mr. Radcliffe's bodyguards. Frank alerted the man to be on the lookout for a tall attractive Chinese lady who may be armed.

"If you show your presence she may be scared away. Please let us handle it. May we use a couple of your radios until morning?" Frank asked.

"No problem," the chief of hospital security said.

Frank walked to the second floor and followed the numbers to Marcus' room. As he opened the door he could see the bed was empty, but then he heard the toilet flush. Marcus exited the bathroom and was startled to see Frank standing there.

"Thank God you're here," Marcus whispered. "I've been afraid to sleep. I was in fear that Nadine had heard the news and would send that person again to kill me."

"Tommy is with me. We'll watch over you until you are released from the hospital, then we will head to the bed and breakfast where you're staying. You can pick up your stuff, and we'll leave the area." Frank said.

"Where's Tommy now?"

"He's parked in the parking area, watching the only entrance. He has a radio to contact me if the Chinese lady shows up. I've alerted the hospital security also." Frank answered.

"You're not going to go anywhere are you?" Marcus asked.

"No, I'll stay right here."

Marcus got back in bed and was asleep in minutes.

Yuke stopped her car a block away from the hospital and walked to the parking lot, staying in the shadows and waited. Another car pulled in and found a parking space near where she was standing. When they exited the car she moved close to them.

Tommy was watching the hospital security car and didn't see Yuke join the couple and their young daughter headed for the entrance with Yuke in step with them. When Tommy looked back at the entrance, he saw what looked like a family with a child entering the hospital's front doors. Once inside, Yuke walked away from the family down a hallway and peered into several doors until she found one with a white hospital smock hanging on a hook. She put it on and picked up a pile of towels to hide her gun. The hospital had only two floors. Each of the patient's rooms had a clipboard outside the door attached to the wall with the patient's information on it in a clear plastic holder.

One by one she checked each room. She had completed the first floor and walked up to the second. There was a hospital employee moping a section of the floor using a yellow and red plastic frame to identify the wet areas. It seemed as if he was taking his sweet time about it.

I need to get rid of that guy

She walked over to him and whispered in his ear,

"I need sex, will you help me?"

The worker put his mop in the bucket and rolled it to

the side of the hallway. He led her to a small room a few feet away and locked the door. As he turned around to face her, she pressed the silencer against his chest and pulled the trigger. He fell in a heap without making a sound. She placed the gun between the towels again and left the room.

A security guard was making his rounds and saw the mop and bucket unattended, He called out the name, Henry, and walked further down the hall and turned the corner. He almost knocked Yuke over.

"Have you seen Henry?", the guard said.

"No."

The guard looked closer at her and said, "Are you new here?"

"Yes," she replied.

"Where is your ID badge?"

"Oh – hold these towels a minute, my badge is in my pocket." The guard reached out for the towels. She pulled the trigger twice and the guard was dead.

Frank thought he heard voices in the hallway. He put down the book he was reading and went to the door and peered out. He saw the guard on the floor and Yuke standing over him.

"Hey! Stop or I'll shoot," Frank shouted. She pointed the gun in Frank's direction and fired two rounds, making Frank duck back into the room. When he looked out again, she was gone. He grabbed his radio and shouted, "Tommy she was here and took a couple of shots at me. I'm okay and so is Marcus. Watch for her to exit the building."

The other guards heard the radio transmission and were all talking at once.

She went out the fire exit at the back of the building and ran into the woods that surrounded the hospital. She made her way around to where she had parked her car, got in, and drove away. "Shit," she said. "Nadine is going to be pissed." Yuke was sure no one had seen her car, and she wasn't about to break any traffic laws on her way back to Nadine's place.

General Chang sent his goons to Yuke's home to find her and bring her back to the Chinese Consulate. His men scaled the wall and broke into the home. They searched the home completely but no Yuke. One of General Chang's men called him and told him she was not there. The General ordered them to burn her house to the ground and return.

"Don't leave any evidence you were even there," he said in a stern voice.

Yuke called Nadine and told her what had happened at the hospital.

Nadine screamed at her.

"You stupid bitch, you can't come back here, and you sure as hell can't go back to your place. Do you have any cash on you?"

"Yes, some," she said nervously.

"Find a place to stay tonight and call me in the morning."

Nadine called Max and asked him to come to the main house. When he arrived Nadine put her arms around his neck and kissed him hard on the lips.

"We have a problem," she said. Nadine explained what Yuke had just told her.

Max's face changed from a smile to a fiery look of anger.

"That dumb bitch is going to fuck everything up for us," he shouted.

"Easy, sweetheart... we'll figure something out."

"Do you think she had any inkling we were playing her?"

"No, not a chance," Nadine answered.

"We can't afford to keep her around any longer. Her government wants her and so does the police... and she may talk" Max said.

"How are we going to do it without being involved?" Nadine asked.

"I have a plan. All we have to do is turn her over to the Chinese government," Max responded, "and she will be on her way to China immediately."

"You think the cops will quit looking for her?"

"In time, yes, I do."

22

Frank and Tommy remained in Marcus' room but out of the way. This gave Frank time to listen to Nadine's cell phone calls – nothing much that he didn't already know. The Tacoma cops were busy marking the location of the brass shells of the two murders. They had already hung the crime scene tape and started their investigation.

Frank told the detective about the attempt on Marcus' life a few days ago. He also said he was sure the person that made the attempt probably saw the news footage as well, and would try again someplace else.

"My partner, Tommy and I, arrived just a few minutes before all this went down. You can check with the hospital security about all that. I'm going to stay here with Mr. Radcliffe until he's released in the morning."

"Do you have anything on the shooter that would help us?"

"No, not really. We think that it's a woman of

Chinese descent and she may work for the Chinese government. At this time that is all I have," Frank said. He didn't want to tell the cops any more than he felt was necessary at this time.

"If you need any follow-up on tonight, here's my card. Give me a call," Frank said.

Marcus had been listening to the conversation and felt safe at the moment. He was sure that with all the law enforcement around, the shooter wouldn't try anything again tonight.

Yuke had stopped at a motel on the south side of Seattle. Once settled in, she called Nadine again.

"I wanted to let you to know where I'm staying," she said.

"Good, stay put for now. I'll call you when I think it's safe."

Max and Nadine knew they had her boxed in. Max put his plan in motion. In the morning he called the Chinese Counsel and asked to speak with General Chang. The person that answered wanted to know what it regarded. Max answered "Yuke Jun." A voice came on the line.

"This is General Chang, how may I help you?" he asked with a thick accent.

"I understand you would like to find Mrs. Jun. I have information that will help you," Max said. Chang's men were busy trying to trace the call, with no luck.

"If this is true, how would it be done and at what cost?"

"I'll take one of your men to the address. Your man would stay close but out of sight. She would recognize me and open the door. Your man would take over, and I would disappear."

"Why would you want to help me?" Chang said.

"I just want her out of my life, and if that's not good enough for you, let's forget about the whole thing," Max said.

"No, no. I'm very interested," Chang said quickly.

"Okay, have your man meet me at The Burger Boy Restaurant on the corner of 38th Ave and Willow Street, this afternoon at five thirty. I'll be standing outside wearing a bright yellow ball cap." Max ended the call.

Max drove to the Burger Boy and waited. He got out of his car at five fifteen and put on his bright yellow ball cap. A few minutes had gone by before an Asian man approached him.

"Do you work for The General?" Max asked. The man nodded.

"Do you speak English?" Again the man nodded.

"Follow me," Max said.

They walked to the front sidewalk, turned right, and continued down the street until they came to a motel. Max walked to room number 112; the Asian man was beside him. Max motioned the man to keep back out of view until the door opened. Max knocked.

Yuke looked out the peephole and saw Max. She opened the door and invited him in.

The Asian man burst in, grabbing Yuke and placed a rag over her mouth. She struggled a bit then went limp from the chloroform. Max dumped her purse. He wanted the keys to her car, the gun, and silencer. When he got what he was looking for he left the room, got into her car, and drove away. Max knew he could pick up his car later.

Another car with two more Asian men pulled into the motel parking area. They entered the room, and waited until dark before placing Yuke's unconscious body in their car and driving into the night toward the Chinese Consulate's main house. Two of the men carried her into the house and back to a room, securing her to a chair. With her chin down on her chest, she finally started to wake up. As her eyes cleared, she noticed that there wasn't any furniture in the room except for the chair she was sitting on. A single light bulb at the top of the ceiling was on, providing the only light. The room had no windows and one door. The floor was concrete. There was a camera and speaker box located at the top of the wall in front of her. She had duct tape over her mouth.

A loud voice from in back of her said, "Mrs. Jun you are at the home of the most gracious General Chang. Are you awake now?"

She nodded.

Two men entered followed by General Chang. The general stood in front of her and told her, "If you give us the information you have about the Radcliffe's latest secret program, we will let you go."

"Dear General, I was friends with Mrs. Radcliffe but she never talked about her business in front of me."

General Chang's face grew tight and twisted.

"I'm no fool, you little tramp. Give us what we want, or you will be sorry." He motioned a man forward. The man held a large, powerful, Taser gun in his hand and pushed the side button. Large sparks between the prongs gave a sizzling sound. She tried to scream but it was muffled by the tape over her mouth.

"Each time we use this on you, it will leave huge scars, and we will continue over and over until that beautiful body of yours is a lump of ugly flesh… do you understand?"

Yuke nodded. Tears were running down her cheeks.

One of the men ripped the tape from her mouth, causing her to cry out.

"Quiet bitch, or I will zap you." She got the message.

"What kind of weapon have they developed?" Chang asked.

She didn't say anything.

Chang frowned, then raised one finger. The man with the Taser gun put it to her neck and pushed the button. Yuke jerked back from the powerful jolt.

"Now you know how it feels. The next time you don't cooperate there will be two jolts, then three, and four. Do you get the picture?"

She was crying and nodded again.

"Now what kind of weapon?"

She was silent. The man stepped forward, and ripped her dress open exposing her bra. He pulled it down and placed the Taser on her right nipple.

"No, no, please… I'll tell you what I know." The man stepped back. She told them what she knew about the weapon named "Green Light," she explained how it operated and what it would be used for. She also said, "There is another project that wasn't completed yet called, "Abilene Gray." I don't know anything about it – only the name."

"Okay, I believe you," Chang said. There is one more question I have for you. Who killed your husband and why?"

"Nadine," She shouted. She wanted him dead so we could be together."

"You have saved yourself from any further torture." Chang raised his gun and shot her between the eyes. Death was immediate.

23

Nadine waited for Max to get back to her house and told him about Yuke's home being burned to the ground.

"It's all over the news," she said.

"Maybe they'll think she died in the fire," Max responded.

Max walked over to the bar near the den and poured himself a stiff drink. He walked back to where Nadine was standing and pulled her close to him.

"I'm never going to share you with anyone again," and kissed her hard on the lips.

She led him to the bedroom and showed Max how appreciative she was.

Now it was Max's turn to find and eliminate Marcus. He reloaded the gun and remade a new silencer. *I'll find you, asshole, and it will be a pleasure putting a bullet in your brain.*

Frank was watching TV, while the hospital staff was preparing to release Marcus.

The commentator announced that the home of the

Chinese Diplomat that was murdered two weeks ago had been burned to the ground.

Frank wondered if she was killed in the fire. The reporter said the fire was determined to be arson, but there wasn't any mention of a body being discovered in the ashes.

Frank, Tommy, and Marcus headed north toward Seattle. As Frank drove, they all talked about what Marcus should do next. Marcus spoke up and said he wanted to get a new Ford Edge with all the bells and whistles.

"Do you have enough cash on you?" Frank asked.

"Yes, I do. I'll need to replenish it soon after the purchase though, if I'm going to stay in hiding."

"You know Nadine will know where you were at the time of the purchase," Frank said.

"Yeah.., I'm getting tired of being on the run. I want to get back to my company and back to work. I have government contracts to finish."

They pulled into a Ford Dealership in South Seattle. A salesman was standing at their car before they had come to a complete stop.

"The gentleman in the passenger seat is interested in a new Ford Edge," Frank said.

Marcus got out of the car and the salesman first question was "what color were you looking for?"

"Red," Marcus replied.

"I'll see what we have in inventory. I'll be right back." Five minutes later he pulled up next to us in a new red Ford Edge.

"Do you have a trade in?" the salesman asked.

"No," Marcus said.

"Do you need financing?"

"No – it will be a cash sale," Marcus answered.

The salesman and Marcus went inside to finish the paperwork. A lot boy drove the red Edge away for a quick wash job and a gas fill-up. He returned with the SUV and placed a temporary-plate on the rear of the car. Minutes later Marcus and the salesman came out to go over all the functions of the new SUV.

"Where do you want your license plates sent to?"

Marcus looked at me with a blank stare.

"Mail them to my house," Tommy quickly said.

"Yes, that will be fine," Marcus replied.

The salesman wrote down Tommy's address and shook Marcus hand. Thank you so much," he said and walked back inside.

"I'm starved, let's go to one of those places that serves breakfast all day," Tommy said.

"Sounds like a plan. After that we have to find a branch of Marcus' bank, so he can make his withdrawal. We should talk about where he will go next."

"After I get the money, I'm going back to the bed and breakfast where I was staying and get my stuff... You know, maybe I'll continue to stay there for a while longer."

"It's hard moving around without Identification," Frank said.

Tommy said, "There's this guy I arrested a year ago that was in that business and I think he's out now. He doesn't know I'm not a cop anymore. Maybe I could tell him he would be helping the cops if he did a special set of ID's for me. Hey, Mr. Radcliffe, stand up and come with me for a minute." Tommy stood Marcus against a blank wall and took a close-up picture of Marcus. They returned to the table just as their food had arrived.

"That is a great idea, Tommy. He will be freed up to take a flight or a cruise or to travel anywhere he wants to, but remember I didn't have anything to do with this," Frank responded.

Nadine was on her computer busily working on business-related issues and a red flag appeared in the upper right hand corner flashing on and off. It was telling her she had an urgent e-mail message. She stopped what she was doing and checked. The new message was from their bank notifying her of a large withdrawal from the business account at a branch of their bank, in south Seattle. Nadine decided not to close the account earlier because it may serve her better in keeping track of Marcus.

That is the second one hundred thousand dollar

withdrawal he's made in the last two weeks. Each of the two one hundred thousand dollar withdrawals by Marcus pissed her off, but it did give her a lead to his whereabouts. She contacted Max and brought him up to date where the withdrawal had been made without telling Max the amount.

Max had just returned from picking up his car from the burger joint near where Yuke had been taken by Chang's men.

General Chang contacted the Seattle Police Department and requested to speak to Detective Tyree.

"Hold on sir, I'll transfer your call."

"Detective Tyree here."

"This is General Chang for the Chinese Consulate," Chang announced in a stern voice.

"Hello General, how can I help you?" Tyree said in an equally stern voice.

"I wanted you to know that we found the man responsible for Wang Jun's murder."

"Oh, that's good news. Who and where is he?"

"His name is Ling Chow and he is on his way to China to stand trial for his crime. He worked for our government as an interrupter and confessed to his involvement.

"You must return him here to stand trial in the United States," Tyree said with anger swelling up within him.

Tyree knew this was a bunch of bullshit, but his

hands were tied. The state department would have to intercede if they really wanted Mr. Ling Chow back, or even if there was such a person.

"General, doesn't it seem strange to you that Wang Jun was murdered, his house was burned to the ground, and his wife, Yuke, is now missing? And, all this happened in a three week time period?"

There wasn't any answer from General Chang, just a buzzing sound from the phone letting detective Tyree know the call had ended.

Above my pay grade Tyree thought.

He put the hand set back on the cradle, and raised his middle finger on his right hand and pointed it at the phone with a slight upward gesture.

My dad once told me, "If you wrestle with a turd the more you will stink." I think he was right.

24

Tommy met Marcus at the bus depot in Lynnwood, Washington, where he gave Marcus his new set of ID's. There wasn't much conversation, just that Marcus would keep Frank posted if he made any changes of his location. Marcus wanted to get back to work so badly – that was just about all he thought about. Nadine still worried him. *What would she do next?*

He decided to stay at the B&B for now. Its location hadn't been compromised at this point, and he enjoyed it there. His new name was Martin Rollins but he wouldn't use it until he had to.

A few of Marcus' employee's had asked about Mr. Radcliffe's absence. Nadine made up a story about him traveling overseas on a business trip. She informed them he was scheduled to be home in about a week. She intended to drain both bank accounts by then. Hopefully, Max would have found him and put a bullet in his brain before Marcus depleted their account.

Max had a quick temper and a dislike for Marcus

ever since Marcus refused to give Max a raise for service to the company. His first payback to Marcus was when he made a play for Nadine and bedded her rather easily long before Yuke came into the picture. Now that she is no longer around and Marcus is on the run, he had positioned himself for an enormous payday. Max's early history began after graduating from college with honors. He joined the Army as a second lieutenant and was assigned to the elite army rangers unit. After six years, his temper got him into trouble more than once. The army brought charges against him for severely beating an enlisted man, which got him a dishonorable discharge. Max went on to work in the electronics field and finally started his own security firm.

Now he was on a mission to find and kill Marcus Radcliffe. He had to do this while out-witting the private investigator, Frank Martini, who was trying to protect Marcus.

The first thing Max found out was that Marcus had purchased a new vehicle, and the Department of Motor Vehicles had an address of 217 N. Broadway in Seattle where the registered owner lived. He really doubted that was where Marcus was staying, but for some reason Marcus gave that address. Max decided to go sit on that address and see who was coming and going.

Tommy's car was parked in the driveway when Max pulled up. He quickly wrote down the plate number and vehicle description.

I'll have my source run it and see if that leads to something. Max dialed a number.

A man answered in a deep base voice.

"Maxie baby, what can I do for ya?"

"I've got a plate for you to run," Max responded.

"Sure, not a problem, how quick do ya need it? Is tomorrow, okay?"

"Yeah, and do a background on the owner too," Max said.

"I'll call ya in the morning."

"Okay," Max said, and ended the call.

The next morning Max was having breakfast when his cell phone went off. The display showed it was Al Darrow, the guy he called last night about running a plate.

"What do you have for me Al?"

"You're not going to believe this, Maxie," Al said laughing.

"Cut the comedy act Al… what gives?"

"The plate comes back to Tommy Saliman."

"So, who the fuck is he?"

"He's a retired cop from Seattle PD."

"You're shitting me," Max said.

"Na, swear to God. He retired last week."

"Thanks Al, I'll drop by your office and we can settle up in the next couple of days," Max said and hung up.

Max told Nadine he wouldn't be around for the next few days, because he had a possible lead on Marcus. She kissed him on the lips and said, "Good hunting, darling."

Nadine had a feeling of relief now that Yuke was gone, and she didn't have to attend to her any longer. She didn't mind the sex part; in fact it was enjoyable... more so than what she had told Max. Being a man, the thought of her with another woman was exciting and he would have liked to have participated. Nadine told Max she had to force herself and act like she was the dominate one, but in reality Yuke *was* the dominate partner.

I will always remember Yuke's smooth pale skin and her soft lips... but enough of this reminiscing, I've got to attend to business. Our company's production has fallen behind.

25

Before Nadine left for work she went to her library, opened the door to the secret room, and checked on the plans for "Green light. They were right where she had left them. *I don't want Marcus to get his hands on these and take them to a place out of my control. My financial future depends on my ability to produce them at time of a sale. Perhaps it would be a good idea if I found another secure location for them.*

This was the only complete set of plans that existed, even Max didn't know about them. She had only let him in on the fact that she had something very secret she wanted to sell, and that Marcus would never go along with it. She told Max that if he would help kill Yuke and Marcus, she would give him five million dollars cash. Max agreed to the deal, and promised he would leave the country and never return when the job was completed.

Nadine had uncovered some very damaging information concerning Max that would insure he would leave the country. She was playing him just like she played everyone in her life. It was all about her.

Nadine's plan was to sell "Green Light" to the highest bidder, then sell her business and disappear forever a rich and single woman.

Frank's office was three miles away from Tommy's house and that was where Tommy was headed. He put the package from the DMV on the seat beside him and backed out of the driveway. Being a former cop, Tommy was always aware of his surroundings. When he reached the street and started toward his destination, he noticed a black SUV pull out a half block behind him. Two miles later it was still there. He decided to make a few unnecessary turns and see if the SUV followed. It did. Tommy called Frank.

"Hey boss, I'm on my way to the office with the new plates for Marcus and I'm sure I'm being tailed by a black SUV."

"How close are you?" Frank asked

"About a mile"

"Pull to the curb, stop, and see what happens," Frank said.

Tommy did as Frank asked and the SUV did the same, about four car lengths behind.

"What's going on?" Frank asked.

"I did and he did," Tommy answered.

"Are you packin?"

"Always," Tommy responded.

"If you feel safe, walk back toward him holding up your retirement badge. He won't know the difference between an active badge and yours. Challenge him and see what he does. If he bolts, get a plate number. If he cooperates get his ID. I'll stay on the line with you. In fact, use your phone like you are running wants and warrants on him and his vehicle."

"Ten-four, Sarge."

Tommy exited his vehicle and started walking back to the SUV, badge in one hand and his cell phone in the other. The windows of the SUV were darkened to the point he couldn't see the occupants inside. Tommy walked up to the driver's side window and rapped on it with his cell phone. The driver's door swung opened hard and knocked Tommy off balance, causing him to fall to the asphalt, badge and phone flying. The driver hit the gas and sped away without Tommy getting a glimpse of the driver or a plate number.

Tommy got up and brushed himself off, gathered his phone and badge, and walked back to his car nursing a sore knee.

He was pissed at the fact he didn't use officer safety that all officers are taught.

That son of a bitch is going to pay when I get my hands on him.

He tried to call Frank, but his phone had been damaged when it hit the asphalt and wouldn't work.

Using a lot of different streets to get to Frank's office,

he was sure he had not been followed. Tommy explained to Frank the problem he had on is way, all the while rubbing his sore knee. Tommy handed Frank the plates for Marcus' new car.

"Wait a minute Tommy." Frank opened the big drawer of his desk. "I have a couple extra burner phones. I'll let you borrow one."

"Thanks, boss," Tommy said.

"Not a problem, "I'm going to call Marcus and set up a place to meet. I want you to make sure that asshole isn't tailing me." Frank said. Marcus answered on the second ring.

"I have your new plates, and I'll bring them to you within an hour." He suggested a meeting place and Marcus agreed. Frank and Tommy mapped out the route they would take.

"When we arrive, I want you to stay back and out of sight to see if the mysterious black SUV shows up."

26

Frank parked near the entrance and went inside. Marcus was seated in a booth in the back. Frank handed Marcus his new license plates and sat down.

"How have you been since the last time I saw you?"

"I'm all healed up and I've met someone to pass the time with. She works at the place where I'm staying," Marcus said with a smile. "She's the cook, and her name is Jenny."

"That's great, but you know Nadine and now Max is looking for you. I hope you haven't told this person anything about yourself including your name, have you?"

"No, I signed in under the name of Martin Rollins when I first registered at the Bed and Breakfast."

Frank's phone rang. The display showed it was Tommy.

"Yeah, what's up?"

"The same SUV pulled in," Tommy said in a whisper. "He's getin' out I think he's headin' inside."

Frank stood up quickly and grabbed Marcus by the

arm. "Follow me", he demanded. Marcus grabbed his new plates, and they ran into the restaurant's kitchen.

Max walked up the steps, opened the door to the restaurant, walked in slowly, and passed the young girl standing at the podium.

"May I help you?" she asked.

Max kept walking looking from left to right as he continued down each isle.

Tommy knew just what to do while Max was inside, and he knew there wasn't much time to do it in. Tommy pulled up to the black SUV, stopped, left his car running, and got out. He quickly reached into his pocket and produced a six-inch knife blade, opened it, and plunged it into each of the four tires on the SUV. Tommy could hear the high-pitched hissing coming from each tire as they were going flat. He went back to his car and drove away.

Frank and Marcus left the kitchen and went out the back door. Tommy came around to the back of the restaurant, picked them up, and drove away laughing to himself at what he had done to the SUV. After learning of Tommy's prank, Frank was pretty sure Max would have to call a tow truck, so he may be there for a while. An hour later the tow truck with a flatbed arrived and hoisted Max's SUV into place. Max got into the passenger's seat of the tow truck with a very upset look on his face and off they went. Tommy drove back to the restaurant and let Frank and Marcus out to retrieve their cars.

"See what I mean about being super careful?" Frank said to Marcus. "I have no idea how that jerk knew where we were, unless he put a tracking device on either Tommy's or my car." Frank checked each vehicle. Sure enough, Tommy's car had one attached to the leaf springs. He detached it from the car and dropped it off at a service station, placing it in a dumpster. If Max wanted to follow it any further, it would lead him to a landfill somewhere outside of Seattle.

Max never got a glimpse of Marcus, Frank, or whoever butchered his tires, but he knew Tommy was there because of the tracking device.

Max called his friend Al Darrow, who had given him information on Tommy's address.

"I need some information on another guy. His name is Marcus Radcliffe. He just bought a new car and I need the make, model, color, and plate number."

"You haven't paid me for the other one yet," Al said.

"For Christ sake, Al, that was just yesterday. You know I'm good for it."

"Yeah, I'll get right on it, I'll call you within an hour," Al said and hung up. Fifteen minutes later Max's phone lit up, the display showed Al Darrow was calling.

"What'd you come up with, Al?"

It's a Ford Edge, red and the plate reads YFN-9336. No more until I get paid."

"Yeah, yeah, yeah," Max said before he disconnected.

27

Frank and Tommy had gone back to the office. Frank noticed Tommy was limping.

"The damn thing has swollen up... maybe I ought to see a doc," Tommy said.

"That's a good idea. If you are unable to work, I'll have to find another guy," Frank said grinning.

"Up yours," Tommy responded. "I've pulled your ass out of rough spots a few times."

"Yep, you sure have. You remember that time when you dared me to walk into the biker bar and challenge the leader to an arm wrestling contest?"

"Yeah," I sure do.

"And the leader called his biggest badass biker over and said I want you to meet Brutus. Brutus was smiling, showing he didn't have two of his front teeth. He was at least six foot, four inches and about two eighty, a bit of a pot belly, long dirty hair with a do rag, and an equally long beard. The biker leader said Brutus was going to stand in for him, and he was going to break my fuckin' arm off and hand it to me."

"Well, if you can have a stand in then so can I."

"Then you called me on the radio and asked me to come into the bar," Tommy said.

"Yeah, and if I remember right you broke Brutus's arm and he was crying like a baby," Frank responded. "We're damn lucky we weren't sued on that one," Frank said. They both were laughing so hard tears were rolling down their faces. For a minute Tommy even forgot the pain from his knee.

"Get your butt to a doctor, big man, and let me know what the results are. I'll pick up the charge," Frank said. Tommy walked to his car and took off for his doctor.

The tow truck took Max's SUV to Bob's Discount Tire, unloading the SUV and Max. The tire shop replaced the four tires within an hour. While he was waiting, Max knew his main mission was to kill Marcus as soon as possible. He would deal with the two retired cops later.

Max drove to Nadine's house and as soon as he walked through the door Nadine asked if the new lead on Marcus had work out.

"Well, yes and no," Max said.

"Tell me the yes part," she asked.

"I got a hold of the information on Marcus's new vehicle. It's a red Ford Edge, and the plate number is YFN-9336.

"Is that it?" Nadine asked.

"No, I was following the big retired cop and he made me. The next thing I know he was standing at my car door tapping on my car window. I opened the door hard and knocked him off his feet. He went down hard, then I took off like a bat out of hell. I'm sure he didn't see me or get my plate number." Max went on to tell her about what happened to his tires and the rest of the story. She had a smile on her face, but didn't say anything, because Max had fire in his eyes. He checked on the device he left on Tommy's car. It was still working and in the same general area as the restaurant, where his tires were slashed.

"I don't think there is any use following the big ex-cop. I'm sure Frank Martini is the only person who knows where Marcus is hiding. I'll see if I can put a tracking device on Martini's car and maybe we can get somewhere.

"I had an interesting morning also," Nadine said.

"Oh, what made it so interesting?"

"A Chinese man who called himself, Ping Chao called me at work. He said he would like to meet with me regarding some very important business." He gave me a contact number, and told me to let him know a date, time and place where we could meet."

"I would guess they must have tortured Yuke until she told them all about "Green Light and now they want to get their hands on it." Nadine felt she should meet with Ping but she didn't feel completely safe. After all, she had no idea if he was an agent for the FBI or an agent for a foreign government.

In truth Ping Chao wasn't his real name. He and his wife came to the United States fifteen years ago from China as a sleeper cell. They became Americans citizens the year after they arrived in the US. They now have two teenage children who have no idea their parents are secretly working for the Chinese MSS (Ministry of State Security). Ping and his wife own a dry cleaning business as a cover.

General Chang had no idea the family even existed. Chang had passed on the information Yuke gave or you could say was forced to give onto the MSS.

28

"**M**aybe you should go in my place", Nadine said to Max. "I have always thought the Chinese males didn't have much respect for women. We could always have him come here. We could use the conference room after the workers have gone home. I'm sure the first meeting with Ping will be a feeling out process. I would feel safer on our own turf."

Nadine's face had a worrisome look, as she glanced at Max. "This may be our big payday." Max reached over and placed his hand on hers and said, "Don't worry sweetheart, I'll handle it." He noticed her hands were ice cold.

That matched her heart.

Max had a weekly sweep of the building done as a routine security check to prevent anyone from recording anything or video-taping. Marcus had a metal detector installed at the entrance of the conference room as an added protection several years ago. The CIA also had very stringent requirements that had to be in place in order to satisfy the government security checks for all vendors.

⸺◦●●◦⸺

Nadine contacted Mr. Ping by the phone number he had given her. She requested they meet tomorrow at 6 PM in her business conference room.

"I will have my chief of security meet you at the front gate. His name is Max, and he will stand in for me. Please be prompt. Do not attempt to record our conversation during our meeting or there will not be a second meeting."

Ping agreed to Nadine's demands and after a short conversation they ended the call.

From Nadine's minds-eye she pictured him as a small man with an easy-going personality. Sometimes when you finally meet the person, they are a complete opposite.

Ping and his wife had been trained in the art of espionage and negotiations. Their handler would make the final decisions on all steps to complete the task at hand, if it ever got that far.

Ping arrived and was escorted to the conference room. Nadine was behind the one-way glass, which was a large picture hung inside the conference room. She could see and hear everything going on in the room.

As Mr. Chao and Max took a seat, Max offered Ping a drink.

"No, thank you," Ping said softly with a smile.

"Shall we get started, Mr. Chao?"

"Yes," Ping said with a slow bowing gesture toward Max.

"What sort of business did you want to discus with Mrs. Radcliffe?"

"It is of a very important and sensitive nature." The smile was gone. All that remained was a dead pan look on Pings face.

"How does that relate to our business?" Max asked.

"A former friend of Mrs. Radcliffe, a Mrs. Yuke Jun, mentioned it to General Chang before her departure for China."

"I see… did Yuke enjoy her trip back home?" Max asked.

"She didn't say," Ping said.

"What is the sensitive information she referred to?" Max asked.

"I believe it has something to do with new electronics in traffic signals called "Green Light." I heard that you are intending on selling the plans to the highest bidder."

Ping was being coy with Max, while staring him in the eye. His actions reminded Max of a professional poker player trying to pull a bluff against, "the fish," the worst player at the table.

Both men sat in silence waiting for the other to respond and each knowing the first to speak usually loses.

"You're telling me you are interested in knowing more about a program called "Green Light," Max said.

"Yes Max, that is exactly what I'm saying" Ping Chao said.

"Perhaps you need to tell us how much you are interested in a program like that. Then get back to us. As you may know there are others that also have expressed a favorable interest."

Max escorted the man back to his car and opened the security gate to let Mr. Chao pass through.

It had been nearly three months now since Marcus and Nadine had attended any social events, business friends had called and left email invites for them to one thing or another.

Nadine was doing her best to avoid the invitations with conflicting business dates or being out of town. She knew she couldn't avoid them much longer without raising suspicion.

Marcus was in his room at the bed and breakfast sitting in his easy chair. He was reading a book he had obtained from the Inn's small library. The book was by a relatively new unknown author, but it was an interesting read. The book had several spicy scenes that got his juices flowing. It reminded Marcus that he hadn't made love in nearly a month. Nadine seemed to have lost interest shortly after they were married.

"Now she is trying to kill me. I'm pretty sure our marriage is over, or at least for me it is."

There was a knock on the door, Marcus tensed up and asked, "Who's there?"

A soft female's voice said "It's Jenny, I'm shutting down the kitchen for the evening. I was wondering if you would like me to prepare a snack for you."

"Please come in, Jenny," Marcus stood and Jenny walked in, wearing a white apron over her dress. She smiled and asked, "What would you like?" Marcus noticed how her large breasts were straining to get out from behind that apron.

"I would like a nice cold glass of milk with two slices of cinnamon toast, and the pleasure of your company when you have finished your work." Jenny smiled and said, "I can handle that, Martin."

"Okay, see you in a few minutes...Martin."

Marcus and Jenny had taken long walks along the river behind the B&B several times and enjoyed each other's company, but nothing more than that to this point. Marcus had always been a proper man, with only a few ladies in his life. He had no idea how to start a relationship. Both he and Jenny were about the same age. The difference between Jenny and Nadine was remarkable. Nadine was hard-boiled and inconsiderate. Where Jenny was bubbly, happy, and fun to be around. A soft knock on the door and an announcement, "It's Jenny."

"Come in my dear," Marcus responded, reaching for the tray in her hands.

Marcus placed it carefully on his table.

"Are you able to stay?" Marcus asked.

"I need to change out of my work clothes and freshen up, then I'll be back."

Marcus lifted the silver dome cover from his plate. There was two slices of beautifully prepared cinnamon toast and a small piece of paper with Jenny's red lip print on it and her phone number.

He kissed the print and placed it back on the plate, then ate the cinnamon toast and drank his cold milk. He hurried into the bathroom to brush his teeth, comb his hair, and, for good measure, take a small sip of mouth wash, swirl it around in his mouth, and spit it out.

A few minutes later Jenny appeared, this time she didn't bother to knock. She moved the desk chair over to the table where Marcus was sitting. Jenny looked at Marcus quizzically cocking her head to one side.

"I hope you don't mind but I need to ask you one question. Are you married?"

"Yes, technically, but please let me explain, I was until a short time ago, but now I'm separated and there isn't a chance in hell we would ever get back together. I hope that won't spoil anything that could be between us." Jenny got up from her seat and walked around the table, leaned over to Marcus and kissed him softly on the mouth.

"Wow," Marcus said, "I've been wanting to do that for the last several days."

"I sensed that, but I was waiting for you to take the first step." She went to the window and closed the curtains and locked the door.

"I want you to know this is the first time I have ever done anything like this, and in fact, I could lose my job if it were ever found out. Are you sure you're okay?"

29

"Marcus got up and walked to the bed, turned down the covers, and then went into the bathroom and closed the door. Jenny knew he was being a gentleman, giving her time to undress and get under the covers.

Marcus came out and snuggled in next to her.

"This will be the first time for me in the last twelve years," Jenny said nervously holding the blanket close to her chin.

"I'm nervous too. I hope I don't disappoint you by not being able to perform," Marcus said with a worried look.

"Let's just take it slow and enjoy ourselves," she said.

Slow turned into an exciting love making experience. They were in each other's arms whispering sweet things. Marcus was feeling very proud of himself. In fact he thought he could bring himself to do it again, but he knew it was getting late and Jenny had to leave without being seen.

"Can we get together again soon?" Jenny asked as

they walked to the door.

"As soon as you're able too," Marcus answered while placing a kiss on her cheek.

"I had a wonderful time... you're a sweet man" Jenny said.

"And you made me feel like a real man again," Marcus replied smiling broadly.

Jenny turned and left, waving goodbye. Marcus stood near the closed door thinking how good he felt and reminisced the evening's events.

His thoughts returned to Nadine. How was he going to explain Nadine to Jenny, and what had taken place lately in his life. He knew that he might have to leave the B&B at any time. He didn't want to hurt Jenny and he didn't want her to get mixed up in the cat and mouse game either.

Marcus called Frank on his burner phone. "Leave a message and I'll call you back," the recorder said. "Give me a call when you get this message," Marcus said.

Frank had been on another line with a potential new client discussing his problem with a cheating wife. Frank told him his top investigator, Tommy Saliman, would contact him a.s.a.p.

Frank called Marcus back immediately.

"What's up, my friend?"

"Frank, we have to end this soon. My business is suffering and living like this, although comfortable, is not me. They know you are helping me. Why can't we offer Nadine an equitable buyout from the company and a monthly stipend for three years?"

"What about the plans for Green Light?" Frank asked.

"She can keep those copies that are hidden in the secret room off the library, and I'll keep mine" Marcus chuckled." Frank knew what he meant and smiled to himself.

"If that's what you want, I'll give it a try." Frank answered.

On the third ring a woman's voice answered. "M&N Biotech Industries, how may I direct your call?"

"Mrs. Nadine Radcliffe, please."

"Whom shall I say is calling?" the voice said.

"Please tell her it's Frank Martini. She should recognize the name," Frank responded.

"Thank you, please hold." The hold lasted several minutes before Nadine answered. Frank was sure Nadine had spoken to Max before she would accept his call.

"Mr. Martini, this is an unexpected call." Her voice sounded sharp and ice cold.

"Yes, I can imagine it is," Frank said slowly and purposefully.

"You called, so what is it you need. I don't have all day," Nadine said.

Now I know why the name nasty Nadine was the employee's favorite.

"Marcus asked me to call, to see if you would be willing to agree to a divorce. He would be willing to buy you out of the company and the marital assets plus a monthly stipend of $10,000.00 for three years."

"Interesting," she said. "What about any of our in-house projects that have not been sold?"

"I'll have to ask Marcus, and get back to you," Frank answered.

She didn't even say goodbye, just hung up. Frank called Marcus.

"At least she is thinking about it," Frank said.

"I'm sure she would like to get this bullshit over with, and if I know her, she will give us an answer within two days."

"Yeah, and if we threw her another big bone, I think she would go for it."

"What do you have in mind Frank?"

"Well, how about some sort of document holding her harmless for the attempts on your life, and also to never disclose any information on her involvement in the murder of Wang Jun."

"Not a bad idea," Marcus said.

Nadine was thinking about the proposal. She was thinking about it very hard.

"Let's see if I've got it straight, we'll split the community property and furnishings. He'll pay me fifty percent of the

value of the business, plus a monthly fee of ten thousand for thirty-six months. He also offered me exclusive rights to "Green Light" and "Abilene Gray." I wonder what else I could ask for. He's bargaining for his life. I've got him right where I want him, between a rock and a hard spot. Nadine's line buzzed again.

Max was on the line.

"Don't take the deal," he said sharply.

"What!"

"The deal Marcus is offering you – don't take it," he said again.

"How the hell? Are you tapping my phone?"

"That's part of my job – to keep you safe."

"The hell it is!" Nadine screamed.

"You take the taps off my personal and office phone immediately," still screaming.

That son of a bitch is out of control, I'll fix that asshole. It helps me make a decision on what I should do about Marcus.

Nadine called Rodney Ashland, her attorney and set up an appointment to meet with him in one hour. She checked the office safe to see the amount of cash on hand.

There were twenty five neatly wrapped bundles of one thousand dollars each. Nadine quickly placed them in a sack for safe keeping, hiding the sack under the spare tire in the trunk of her car until she could find a better location. She went to Rodney Ashland's office. Rodney had his secretary clear his calls and appointments for the rest of the day.

"I'm thinking about divorcing Marcus or should I say, he wants a divorce and he has offered a settlement of assets." Nadine went on laying out the offer, minus the part about her killing Wang Jun.

"To tell you the truth Mrs. Radcliffe, it's a generous offer, but there may be additional monies to be had." Ashland could smell a large amount of money ahead, especially if he could drag it out for a period of time, and create more billing hours.

Then his balloon deflated when Nadine said Marcus wanted this agreement to be settled quickly. The smile on Rodney's face went placid.

"Would I be representing represent both parties?"

30

"**H**ell no! He'll have to contact someone of his own choosing," she said with an angry smirk spreading across her face. "Don't screw this up." Nadine said to Rodney. "I want out of this marriage as badly as he does, for reasons I don't want to get into now."

"Okay, let's go over the family assets first, then we will discuss your business and establish a value."

For the next hour and a half they went over everything. Rodney asked if Marcus was living at home.

"No, not currently. He's been traveling." Nadine didn't add any additional information to Rodney's question.

"In the meantime, I'll do some probing to see if Marcus has any hidden bank accounts, stocks, bonds, or other investments,"

"That would be appreciated. Call me with any results," Nadine said.

Nadine stood, they shook hands, and she walked out of Rodney's office. His eyes watched her. *Such a beautiful woman, soon to be available again. I wonder if there's someone else involved.*

Nadine walked to the parking garage, up to the second floor, and down the aisle to where she had parked. There was Max leaning against the back fender of her car. It startled her at first, then she lit into him, calling Max every dirty name she could think of.

"First my phones and now my car. I suppose you have a tracking device on it somewhere. Take it off right now damn you, take it off!" Max got down on his knees, reached under the frame and removed a small device with a red light blinking.

"One more stunt like this, and I'll fire your damn ass," Nadine said angrily.

"I don't think that will ever happen, bitch. I've got so much shit on you," Max shot back.

Oops, the spoken word was out and can't be taken back, but that is the way he felt down deep. His anger got out of control in the military and cost him dearly, this time it may cost him also.

Nadine knew he was right. The question was. *Is he going to live long enough to tell anyone?*

She got into her car and slammed the door. She left the parking garage with her foot on the accelerator and tires squealing. Max knew he was right, but he also knew she was the one with the money and he needed to make amends with her damn fast.

Max followed her to her home. He tried to call her on

his cell phone but she wouldn't answer. He left a message telling her how sorry he was and would like to make it up to her. He ordered flowers to be delivered to her, then drove to his office and waited for a call from Nadine.

The gate opened, the florist truck drove to the home's entrance, and the delivery person rang the bell. Nadine opened the door and accepted the large beautiful bouquet. The truck drove away. Nadine went to the kitchen and promptly threw the flowers into the trash bin.

If you think you're going to buy me off that easy, you're way off base buster. You've way over-stepped the line. Maybe you have forgotten – you work for me – not the other way around.

Nadine knew there would come a time when she would no longer need Max, and that time was drawing nearer. Earlier, Nadine and Max had devised a plan to dispose of Marcus' body.

Now there may be no need to kill Marcus, she thought. Perhaps she could use the same plan on Max.

Nadine decided she would offer Max a chance to make up. She would invite him to dinner and flirt with him until he wanted sex. Afterwards, she would offer him a poisoned drink, killing him instantly.

The rest of the plan would already be in place. It was simple. She would hire two men to buy a medium sized tree shredder and lumber. They would bring it to the back wooded section of her property and build a wooden box large enough to wheel the shredder inside later. Next they would place the shredder on an extra-large plastic tarp. The men would take Max's naked body to the shredder, dismember it, and run the body parts through the shredder.

The mangled remains would be on the tarp. The men would roll the shredder into the box and seal it. They would pull the plastic together and seal it also. With the use of a large rental truck that had a lift gate, the boxed-up shredder and the plastic trap would be loaded on the truck and taken to a dock on the water and put aboard a boat. When they were three miles out, the men would cut a one-foot square hole in each side of the wooden box. This would allow small fish to get inside to eat the remaining flesh left on the shredder. The tarp would be opened while on the boat and washed clean of Max's remains, then dumped into the sea. On their way back to shore Nadine would shoot her two accomplices, and dump their naked bodies overboard. She was hoping that law enforcement would see it as a gangland shooting when they washed ashore. This would be done at night.

Now the only change in the plan is it would be Max instead of Marcus.

The two things yet to do was find the two men to help.

31

Twenty-four hours had passed since Frank contacted Marcus.

"No word from your wife yet, do you want to sweeten the pot?"

"No, I will wait another twenty four hours, then you can contact her and mention the document I would give her – the one holding her harmless for the attempts on my life, and the original recordings of her admission of killing Wang Jun along with the video of her having a sexual affair with his wife. If that doesn't do it, nothing will," Marcus said while staring out the large window the of B&B'S dining room.

Marcus and Frank finished their conversation. Marcus tapped a contact button on his phone. Jenny came on the line. "Sorry can't talk now, I'm decorating a cake. Can I call you later?"

Jenny didn't have Marcus's cell number. What she meant was she would call his room number. Marcus left the dining room and walked to his room to wait for Jenny's call. Marcus answered on the first ring. *Maybe it seemed a little too anxious,* he thought.

"Hello," he answered.

"Hi, it's Jenny."

"How about dinner and a movie after work?" Marcus asked.

"Like a real date?"

"Yes, like a real date," Marcus answered.

"I'll give you my address. You can pick me up at 6:00 PM."

Marcus searched the paper for a suitable movie and a nice restaurant.

He noticed a movie called "The Country House," that started at 6:30 and a seafood restaurant, "The Daily Catch." He dialed and made a reservation for 9:00. Marcus was hoping they would find time for intimacy before the night was over. Marcus got his wish.

─◆◆◆◆─

When Marcus bought his new car, he not only gave the salesman Tommy's address, he also used Tommy's email account. Everyday there was emails and snail mail from the dealership. Thanking Marcus for his business or offering him additional services. Tommy just deleted the email and took the postal mail to Frank. Frank put it in a plastic grocery bag and planned to deliver it to Marcus the next time they hooked up.

Marcus didn't seem like the same guy Frank met at the spa a month ago. His demeanor was much more relaxed and now he smiled and laughed occasionally. But he missed his business and yearned to get back to it – especially if Nadine was no longer a partner.

"Tommy, how are things going with the domestic case I gave you the other day?"

"Pretty good, boss. I got some pictures of the wife on her knees with the guy she works for. I'm waiting until I can get a shot or two of them doing the nasty," Tommy said.

"If she is on her knees now it won't be long before they're in bed together," Frank said.

"The funny thing is boss, when I showed the husband the pictures, it seemed to excite him more than piss him off. Go figure, huh?"

"You'll run into all kinds in this business," Frank responded.

Frank's cell phone buzzed, the display showed it was Marcus." "Good afternoon Marcus," Frank said.

"Yes, it is," Marcus replied in a cheerful voice. Any word from Nadine?"

"No sir, all is quiet."

"Okay, I have drafted a short document as we discussed. Tell her to contact Rodney Ashland concerning the divorce and assets. I will find someone to represent me. This current document will be signed and dated by her and me, and witnessed by Max and you...Frank. It will not be mentioned in the divorce settlement. Frank, I want you to call her and set up a meeting for today, to present this information at a secure location of your choosing. You can also tell her I need to have her final answer by 5:00 PM tomorrow. Now's here's the draft."

Frank copied it word for word.

"I'll call her as soon as we hang up," Frank answered.

"I'll talk with you tomorrow," Marcus said and left the line.

Frank dialed Biotech Industries and again he asked for Mrs. Radcliffe, repeating his name for the receptionist. Nadine answered and immediately said, "Let me call you back on a secure line," and hung up. Two minutes passed before Frank's cell buzzed. "Mrs. Radcliffe can we meet somewhere of your choosing? I have more information for your ears only."

32

"Yes, I'll meet you in an hour at your office." Her choice of a meeting place surprised Frank, but he agreed and hung up.

Frank got busy straightening the office to make it look professional, but it would take more than straightening to accomplish that, he realized, and gave up. He was not going to engage Nadine in conversation any more than necessary.

Forty-five minutes later there was a light tap on his door. Frank stood from his desk, walked to the door, and opened it. The beautiful Nadine Radcliffe stood in the archway and held out her hand. To Frank it seemed like the female black widow inviting the male to have sex before she kills him. Frank waved his hand toward the desk chair without touching hers. She smiled a sly come-hither smile. They took a seat. There was a file folder on top of the desk.

"Would you care for a drink, Mrs. Radcliffe?" Frank said with a dry throat.

"Only if you have one with me," she countered.

Suddenly Frank thought the room was getting warm. He stood and walked to the middle of the room and pulled on the chain to the old ceiling fan. It clanked a couple of times and the blades started turning. "I think I'll pass on the drink," Frank said.

He turned, walked back, and sat down at his desk. Frank acted like he didn't notice she had used his first name.

"Let's get down to business," Frank said opening the file in front of him.

"You no doubt remember the various things Mr. Radcliffe offered you in our last conversation." She nodded and waited for Frank to continue.

"Mr. Radcliffe would like to add two additional things outside of the divorce. One is for you and the other is for him." Nadine sat straight in her chair and with her right hand she adjusted the hem of her dress to mid-thigh showing more leg than necessary. She smiled, crossed her legs, and said, "Let's hear it."

"First, your husband would like you to agree to a no-compete agreement that will last for fifteen years. Also it would encompass a radius of 1,500 miles."

"That's acceptable. What is the one thing you think would be to my benefit?" Nadine asked.

"Mr. Radcliffe has drafted a document that will hold you harmless for your involvement in the attempts on his life, and the information he has implicating you in the murder of Wang Jun. It would require both yours and his signatures. The document would be witnessed by myself and your security chief, Max Neal."

Nadine laughed and leaned back in her chair, "You have to be out of your fucking mind. I haven't been involved in any of those things."

"You must know by now that we have audio and video of your involvement," Frank said.

"Then why haven't you gone to the police to have me arrested? I'll tell you why – the information you gathered was obtained illegally and would be inadmissible," She said with a gotcha smirk on her face.

"Maybe you're right at this time, but we could turn it over to the cops, and they would start an investigation causing you and Max a world of hurt. The investigators would dig into everything about you, Yuke, and Max. In no time they would have a case put together and the DA would bring you to trial. You both would go to prison for a long time, maybe even life. One other thing… we know about Yuke also," Frank said with the same kind of smirk. That was bullshit but she didn't know that.

"I'll have to think about it," Nadine responded

"You have until 5:00 PM tomorrow or the offer is off the table."

"Everything?" she asked.

"Everything," Frank replied.

"Maybe I'll call your bluff, and tell you to shove it up

your ass."

"If that's what you want, we'll turn everything over to the cops now, then you can deal with them. Hang on, I'll call Mr. Radcliffe and see what he says." Frank had Marcus's number on speed dial.

Marcus answered. "What is it Frank?"

"Well sir, I feel your wife thinks you are joking, and she said you can shove it where the sun doesn't shine."

"Tell her I'm taking the deadline off the table. She has to make a decision yes or no before she leaves your office today or we hand it over to the authorities." Frank had the call on speakerphone and she heard every word.

"Alright sir, I'll tell her," Frank said.

"There's no need to repeat it. I heard what he said." Her face no longer looked friendly. She stood and began pacing across the room, with a worried look. The window behind Frank's desk was open and the wind had picked up enough to make the papers on his desk fall to the floor. Frank closed the window, looking at the dark clouds that had formed. "Looks like we're in for a hell of a storm," Frank said, as large raindrops began pelting the glass.

"Shit!" Nadine said. My car windows are down. I'm going to run down and close them. I'll be right back."

"If you leave my office, the deal is off, that's what your husband said."

"You can't be serious," Nadine shot back.

"As serious as a heart attack." Frank answered.

Nadine kept pacing and thinking what were her options. *If she accepted all of Marcus's terms, that would change her entire plan. But it would leave her free to sell "Green Light, and not have to share the proceeds with anyone. She could still follow through with killing Max. But she would be free from all of her recent indiscretions. If I don't accept, we'll have to continue the cat and mouse game, with the cops nosing around in my business. With piles of terrible publicity and after a lengthy trial, I'll probably go to prison.*

"Alright Martini, I'll accept his proposal in its entirety."

"Fine, you can go close your car windows, and I will notify Mr. Radcliffe of your decision. You may want to get in touch with your attorney right away," Frank said noticing she was back to using his last name.

"Do you have an umbrella?" Nadine asked.

"No, Mrs. Radcliffe I don't." Frank answered.

"Would you be so kind as to close the car windows for me?"

"Sorry Nadine, that's not my line of work."

Frank walked to his closet and found his raincoat and slipped it on. He grabbed the sack of mail he was delivering to Marcus. Frank followed Nadine out the door and locked it behind him. She was furious at him for addressing her as Nadine and also not helping her with the rain issue.

Frank called Marcus, as a rain-soaked Nadine drove

away. He wanted to explain how the meeting went. Marcus laughed when he heard the part about her car windows and not being able to leave the office until she made a decision.

33

"I have some mail for you, and I'm on my way with it, if you're going to be there." Frank said.

It's raining like hell here," Marcus answered.

"Here, too."

An hour later Frank pulled up to the B&B.

Marcus had been gazing down at the B&B parking lot as Frank drove up. He hurried downstairs to meet him. Marcus extended his hand in friendship. Frank followed his gesture. Marcus led Frank to the large living room, and they each sat in plush leather chairs. Frank retold Marcus about his meeting with Nadine. They each had a good laugh. Marcus looked over the mail Frank brought and discarded it.

"Frank, I want you to meet someone." Marcus dialed a number, said a few words, and hung up. Minutes later an attractive woman appeared from the other end the room. She was dressed in a cook's uniform, complete with the white cap and apron. As she approached, you could see her warm inviting smile. Both men stood.

Marcus said, "Jenny this is my close friend Frank Martini, and Frank I would like you to meet my very special friend, Jenny." They shook hands.

"Can you join us for a few minutes?"

"I'm so sorry Martin, but it's not allowed while I'm on duty but maybe later."

"I thought as much, but wanted to ask," Marcus said holding her hand a little longer than he should. Jenny excused herself and went back to the kitchen.

"I've grown quite fond of Jenny, and I believe she feels the same about me. When this mess with Nadine is over, I want to continue my friendship with her." Marcus said like a little schoolboy who was smitten.

"She seems like a very nice person and quite attractive also." Frank whispered.

Marcus leaned in close and said, "She's the best I've ever had in bed.

"Wow, Marcus you have really changed since the first time I met you at the spa."

"Yes, I was an up-tight ass, and I'm really sorry about that. I guess almost losing my life a couple times has changed the way I look at things now."

"I like the new Marcus... he's fun to be around," Frank said while patting him on the back.

"Let's walk up to my room and discuss the near future," Marcus said.

"Lead the way, boss," Frank answered.

Frank admired Marcus' room – beautifully furnished,

clean, and private.

"Can I offer you a drink? They have a full bar downstairs. I order and they bring it up." Marcus said.

"Two Bloody Marys would hit the spot." Frank responded.

"Two?" Marcus repeated, with a quizzical look.

"Yeah, I'm thirsty," Frank said remembering Vi Holster by the pool in Carmel.

Frank hadn't shared his dalliances with Marcus or anyone else for that matter. They were tucked away in his memory, along with other pleasant thoughts of that weekend.

"Can we trust Nadine to follow through with the plan?" Frank asked Marcus.

"Yes, I'm sure we can. She has everything to gain and nothing to lose."

"Max will be off your ass now and you can go back to your business. I wouldn't stay at the house yet. Let's wait until we are positive you'll be safe." Frank said.

"I was thinking the same thing."

The divorce will cost me an extreme amount of money. I don't know if I will be able to survive financially without a cash infusion, but I have a back-up plan I think will work. Do you remember my good friend Ben Swanson, the owner of a yacht based at the Eagle Yacht Club in Bremerton, WA?"

"Yeah, why?"

"Ben is a very wealthy man, and I think he would be

happy to be equal partners in my business. That would be the cash infusion I need. He would put up half the business's worth and I would run the day-to-day operations. He could continue his retired lifestyle, and we would split the profits."

"Damn, maybe someday I could travel in the circles of the rich and famous," Frank said laughing.

"If our plans work out my friend, you'll be on your way," Marcus quipped.

Frank wasn't sure what Marcus meant, but it sounded good. Their conversation lasted for two hours, before Frank said, "I have to get back to the office and meet Tommy."

34

Nadine called Ping Chao on a burner phone. A woman answered, "Who's calling please?"

"Nadine for Mr. Chao." The line seemed to go dead, then a voice said, "Mr. Chao will meet you in one hour at Broadway and Central in back of Walgreen's. Come alone." This time the phone did go dead. Nadine went to her computer to check how far it was to that particular Walgreen's. She looked at her watch and decided she had plenty of time to make the trip.

Nadine wanted to inform Ping Chao what it was going to cost his government to obtain the "Green Light's plans. She didn't want to negotiate. The price was firm, or she would find another buyer. Fifty million dollars didn't seem like an unreasonable price to her. To the filthy rich Arab oil states, that amount of money is spent at the crap tables in Monte Carlo in a single night.

Mr. Chao showed up right on time, parked, walked to Nadine's car, and slid in the front passenger's seat.

"This shouldn't take long Mr. Chao. The price is $50

million dollars in US currency to be placed in my offshore account in Panama."

"I will have to contact the decision maker in China to verify the purchase agreement. Then, we will need to test the weapon here in the United States. If the weapon performs as you state, you will see a deposit of funds to your Panama account. You will then hand over the working plans."

My God, I just had a brilliant idea. Why not use this test on Max instead of all that shredder bullshit. It will prove that the weapon works on human beings and it will kill Max at the same time. I'll stipulate to the Chinese watching the test that they must get rid of Max's body.

"When can we see a test," Ping asked smiling like the deal had already been accepted.

"I'll provide the test subject. You can take charge of him after the test and keep him in your custody. He will die within 48 hours without any trace of what killed him. Then you can get rid of his body, never to be found," Nadine said coldly.

"Where and when will we perform the test?" Ping asked.

"In the woods on my property. I'll be ready tomorrow evening at 7:00 PM."

"I'll bring a few friends to help with the body. Is that okay with you Mrs. Radcliffe?"

"By all means, Mr. Chao."

Nadine had to figure out how she was going to dupe

Max into being used as the test subject to sell the "Green Light" project.

That evening Nadine went into the chemist lab in her building and found a small vile of a neuromuscular-blocking agent drug. When injected it would cause complete paralysis throughout the body. The person can see and hear what is going on around them, but they are unable to speak or move. The effects of the drugs will wear off in five hours.

Nadine filled a syringe with 200 units, capped it, and then placed it in her pocket. According to the dosage charts 200 units would keep Max immobile for six hours.

Nadine's plan was to entice Max over for dinner, and while he was seated at the table she would walk up behind him and plunge the syringe into his neck. Within ten seconds Max would be completely paralyzed.

Nadine called Max and invited him over for dinner the next night at five PM. He was happy to accept the invitation. Max thought he was back in her good graces again.

Nadine went to her library and opened the door to the secret room. Once inside she retrieved the original "Green Light" model gun they had tested before. Nadine returned to her library and placed it on a chair. She reached into the pocket of her lab coat and removed the syringe. She placed it in a small plastic bag and put it in the refrigerator.

Using her finest china and crystal, she set the table for two, including her favorite wine glasses.

It was a macabre scene, knowing what would happen in less than 24 hours.

At 5:00 PM sharp Nadine's doorbell rang. It was Max. "Please come in," Nadine said purring like a kitten. She was wearing a full-length form fitting black dress with a plunging neckline. Her coal black hair was pulled back into a bun, a single strand of white cultured pearls hung lightly on her neck reaching down to her cleavage.

Max on the other hand was wearing cargo shorts, a faded sport shirt, and sandals that were showing their age.

This uncouth jerk deserves to die.

Max reached out. He put his hands on her shoulders and lightly kissed her on the cheek.

"Dinner is ready Max. Please take a chair at the dining room table."

Nadine hadn't made any dinner. Why should she? Max wouldn't be able to enjoy it in a few short minutes anyway.

Max sat down and Nadine went to the kitchen refrigerator to retrieve the bag with the syringe. She took it out and pulled off the cap, making it ready for use. Holding a bottle of opened wine in one hand and the syringe in the other, she approached Max from the back. She brought the wine from over his shoulder and began to pour. Her other hand found its mark with the syringe. She pushed the plunger hard and emptied its contents into his body. Max jerked, slapped his hand at his neck, and raised out of his chair in one fluid move. Nadine took several steps backwards as Max staggered toward her then collapsed onto the floor, with his eyes wide open. Nadine came close to his body and lightly kicked at him to get a response.

Nothing. She bent down and took his wallet and keys from his pockets.

She was still holding the bottle of wine as she walked back to the other end of the table to her place setting, poured herself a half glass of wine, and sat the bottle down.

35

She looked back at Max and raising her glass in a toast, and said, "I'm a bitch, you were an asshole, and the bitch won. Now, I get the whole pie. There's no one left to split it with." She emptied her glass in one gulp.

Ping Chao and three of his men arrived at the gate. It was 7:00 PM. Nadine buzzed them in, and they drove to the entrance. She opened the door and asked them in.

"Are you ready for the test?" Ping Chao asked.

"Yes, the subject is over there," she said pointing at Max who was still in the same position. Ping's men lifted Max and put him in the trunk of their car.

Nadine picked up the "Green Light" gun and told them to follow her to the wooded area at the back of her property. There was still plenty of light available to complete the test. When they arrived at the spot Nadine had chosen, two of Ping's men stood Max's body up against a large tree and tied a rope under his arms and around the tree. Max could see and hear what was happening to him, but unable to move or speak. Nadine, Ping, and his men walked 200 yards away from where Max was tied.

Nadine told Ping to use his binoculars and focus them on Max's forehead. "When you see a red dot appear, the shot has been completed." Nadine clicked on the weapon's power source, kneeling down on one knee. She raised the gun and using the high power scope, she concentrated the cross hairs on the center of Max's forehead. She pulled the trigger. The only sound was the trigger click. Ping saw the red dot appear for only a second, then it was gone.

Nadine stood and told Ping he will die within 48 hours. "You can take him away now. He will be able to move again in about two hours. When you are satisfied with the test, we will meet again and exchange money for plans."

Ping nodded and his men picked up Max and left.

Max woke up a few hours later and the paralysis was gone. He was in a room with sound-proof padding on the walls. Max knew he had a few hours left to live and was screaming at the top of his lungs. No one could hear him including the guard watching through the thick glass window at the door.

There was a camcorder located in the ceiling. Ping wanted to use the recording to help prove the test worked. Max died sixteen hours later. Ping had a

Chinese doctor check his body for any other causes of death. None were found.

Nadine drove Max's company car to the docks in a rough part of town, parked it, and wiped it down, destroying all fingerprints. She left the keys in the ignition, figuring someone would take it for a joy ride or to a chop shop. She called a cab and was taken back home.

After seeing the recording and viewing Ping Chao's report, the Chinese MSS authorized full payment for the plans to the weapon.

Nadine picked up the binder containing the disks with step-by-step instructions on assembling the weapon and made several copies, just in case she wanted to sell them again. These were the same disks Marcus had compromised a month earlier without her knowledge.

When the money was transferred to her offshore account, Nadine handed Ping Chao the binder of disks. Their business was over, or so she thought.

Ping Chao left for China the next morning with the disks. The MSS were very anxious to get their hands on them. They had been disguised as CD music albums. The MSS had a group of top Chinese scientists waiting at their lab to start their effort to recreate the weapon. Starting with the injected molded plastic frame. Others would tackle the laser, trigger mechanism, and anthrax. The head scientist determined the time to produce the weapon would take at least two weeks. Once assembled, they were going to test it on a large pig.

36

Marcus asked Frank if he thought it would be okay to return to work since Nadine had agreed to everything.

"From what I know, she will be leaving as soon as everything is settled," Frank answered with a smile.

"I'll break the news to Jenny that I'll be moving back to Seattle. In the meantime, let's find a place that I can rent for a week at a time, preferably close to my business."

Frank called one of his past squeezes who was in the real estate business.

"Hi Dotty, Frank Martini here. Do you still work in real estate?"

"Hi honey. Yeah, I still do, what do you need?"

"A classy apartment that rents out weekly on the East side."

"Weekly?"

"Maybe two at the most."

"You have the same number Frank?"

"No, but I can hang on the line, while you check."

"You just don't want me to have your new number do ya," she said laughing. "Don't worry hon, I'm a married woman now. Let me put you on hold." Frank hung on for what seemed like an eternity.

"Sorry for the long wait, but I found just the place for you and it's completely furnished."

The tenant moved out two weeks early on his lease. It's vacant, and I can show it to you right now."

Give me the address and my friend and I will meet you there."

"It's 106 Robin Trail."

"I'll check it out on my GPS. See you in a few," Frank said and clicked off before she could ask about his friend.

"Why don't we both drive, then you won't have to bring me back to the B&B?" Marcus asked.

"Okay by me," Frank answered.

Frank took the lead and followed the GPS directions.

They arrived before Dotty. When she pulled up and got out of her car, she smiled and Frank's jaw dropped, Dotty was as big as a barn, eight months pregnant. She looked like she would drop at any minute. Dotty hugged Frank and kissed him on the cheek. Frank congratulated her, and then introduced Marcus. They all went inside and toured an elegant apartment.

Without hesitation Marcus said "I'll take it. Dotty filled out the paperwork and Marcus handed her enough cash to cover the two weeks. Dotty said goodbye to them and handed Marcus the keys.

"That was quick," Frank said staring at the beautiful furnishings. "When will you move in?" Frank asked.

"Tomorrow evening. I want to spend tonight with Jenny."

"Frank, do you to know how much I depend on you? You are very resourceful man. I trust you above all others." Frank knew it was high praise coming from a man like Marcus.

After Marcus arrived at the B&B, he gathered his belongings and readied them for his departure the next evening. He went to the Office and settled his account, then walked back to the kitchen and peeked in. There were two women working away, but not Jenny. He walked out to the parking lot and noticed her car wasn't there. His heart skipped a beat. *Was she fired, quit, or perhaps sick? Surely she would have let me know.*

Marcus heard a car behind him. It was Jenny's. She parked in her normal space and got out. "Where were you? I was beginning to worry."

"I was at the grocery store shopping for the B&B. I do it every week at this time, dear." She smiled and began lifting sacks of groceries from the trunk. "Let me help you," Marcus said. When all the sacks were on the kitchen counter, he whispered to her, "Please come to my room after you've finished your work. It's very important."

She nodded and whispered to him, "Okay," her

expression was one of confusion.

At 6:00 o'clock Jenny was at Marcus' door. "Okay what's all the mystery about?"

"I want to give you some information, before you hear it through the grapevine." Jenny sat at the small table across from Marcus with her arms resting on the table's edge.

"You've asked me here to tell me you're leaving me, aren't you?"

"Well, yes but only for a short time," Marcus responded.

"That doesn't make any sense to me."

"Please let me explain." Marcus told Jenny the whole story – how Nadine had been conspiring to kill him and take over the business; what his real name was; Nadine's affair with Yuke; how he had hired Frank Martini to keep him safe; and about the divorce between him and Nadine.

"So, is our relationship over?" Jenny asked with tears forming in her eyes.

"No sweetheart, if it was over I would have left without telling you anything. I'm falling in love with you Jenny, I want you to join me when the divorce is final, and that should be in about two or three weeks. If you agree you can give your notice here and join me. We will stay in contact daily."

"Yes, yes, yes," she said. Jenny jumped up and ran to the other side of the table, threw her arms around

Marcus's neck and kissed him all over his face. "Make love to me darling, right here and right now," she said unbuttoning his shirt with shaky hands. She was so excited.

After they were finished Marcus said, "Honey, will you spend the night?"

"Let me go home and get a change of clothes for tomorrow, and I'm yours for the night."

37

The Chinese scientist had completed replicating the weapon in ten days and was ready for testing.

Ping Chao was invited to join the others to witness the test. A team made up of the top twelve biotechnology scientists gathered close around the weapon. They had chosen a large hog for the target. At a range of a quarter mile, one of the top MSS officers a Colonel Ming would do the honor of pulling the trigger. Workmen had constructed a wooden stand to steady the weapon against.

The hog was in place, the weather was perfect, there was no wind or rain. Ming picked up the weapon, turned on the power source and the anthrax capsule ruptured, sending anthrax spores through the air in all directions. All attendees – Ping Chao, Colonel Ming, the twelve scientists and the MSS men were dead within 36 hours.

The hunt was under way for Nadine – the bitch that killed their countrymen and had stolen fifty million dollars from them.

Not knowing what had taken place in China, Nadine was boarding a cruise ship heading to Alaska for the next ten days. She knew Marcus was coming back to work at the company business, and she was just waiting for the divorce to become final.

The MSS had sent three men to find and kill Nadine. They called her company and were told she was on vacation and would return in two weeks.

"Is there any way we can contact her? It's very important."

"I doubt it – she's on a cruise ship headed to Alaska."

The MSS men hacked into the various cruise lines in route to Alaska for a Nadine Radcliffe.

The information popped up on the Princess Line along with her cabin number. The ship's first port stop would be in Ketchikan, Alaska. The cruise lines have very tight security, and the MSS men knew they would have a difficult time getting aboard. They called their contact in Seattle and told them of their problem. An hour later the MSS men received a call back and were told their ID badges for cook helpers would be waiting for them along with three Philippine passports when they arrived in Ketchikan, Alaska. The MSS had hacked into the Princes Line computers and added their names to the crew's list.

—◆◆◆◆—

It was the first night of the cruise and Nadine was seated

at a table for six in the main salon. Soon five others joined her. Each was a passenger traveling alone – three men and three women. The other two women were less attractive by far than Nadine. The men's conversation was directed toward Nadine, making the other women uncomfortable and jealous. The men were buying her drinks and had offered Nadine their company after the dinner was over. She politely declined. It was going to be a 10-day cruise and she didn't want to hook up with anyone that quickly. She felt confident they would be sniffing at her heels until she had picked someone. She knew she would meet several more desirable men or perhaps another woman. She had always thought how fun it would be seduce a happily married woman into her first lesbian affair – someone who was curious but had never acted on it – just like the blonde with large full breasts sitting two tables away. The man with her was drinking heavily. Nadine heard him tell the blonde he was going to the casino and would see her later. *How perfect that would be,* Nadine thought.

Nadine excused herself and walked to the young blonde's table and extended her hand. "Hi, I'm Nadine, may I join you?" The blonde looked up and shook Nadine's hand and said, "Yes, I would love someone's company right now. My name is Casey, Casey Donaldson."

"Was the gentleman that left the table your husband?"

"Yeah, that's him. We booked this cruise three months ago. We've been together for two years and got married this morning at a chapel in Seattle. This is our wedding night and that asshole is spending it at the casino."

"I heard him from over there where I was sitting. I'm traveling alone, and those men at my table keep hitting on me and won't take no for an answer."

"No wonder, you are a very beautiful woman," Casey said in an approving way.

"If I know men, I think your husband will be on his own for the rest of the evening."

"You're probably right," Casey answered.

"Why don't we go and explore the ship and see what is happening this evening."

"We can change into something more comfortable and meet by the large pool on the main deck in thirty minutes," Nadine said.

"See you then," Casey responded. She wanted to have fun and now she had met someone who felt the same way.

They started by checking out all the retail shops, looking at clothes and shoes. Next it was gift shops and the last one they wandered into was a large jewelry store. Casey was admiring a diamond bracelet. Nadine looked over Casey's shoulder, "What a beautiful piece," Nadine said looking directly at Casey. Casey put the bracelet on her wrist held her arm out. The store lights made the diamonds sparkle and come alive.

Nadine said, "We'll take this," to the sales clerk.

Casey looked quizzical. "What are you doing?" she asked.

"This is my wedding present to you, Nadine said.

"What, I don't even know you. You can't do that," Casey said.

"Don't worry, honey, I can well afford it, and it gives me pleasure."

And I'll get the pleasure back from your body with mine later.

"Oh, my God, thank you so much," Casey leaned over and kissed Nadine on the cheek.

Nadine returned the kiss and thought – y*ou and I will be exchanging many more kisses among other things tonight.*

"Let's go dancing at one of the lounges," Nadine suggested, and they were off.

The music was loud and the place was packed. They stood at the entrance and surveyed for a place to sit. A young man approached them and offered to share his table.

He seemed like a clean-cut guy about Casey's age. Nadine and Casey looked at each other and nodded.

They all took a seat at his table, and the young gentleman bought the ladies their first drink. It wasn't long before another man joined them at the table. Two hours had passed with plenty of drinks, dancing, and light fun conversation. The ladies excused themselves to use the ladies room. While in the restroom they were saying how much fun they were having. Casey said she was feeling a little tipsy.

"Go ahead, honey, enjoy yourself. I'll take care of you baby." Casey put her arms around Nadine's neck and kissed her on the lips. "Oops," Casey said. "You're just so damn beautiful. Sorry."

"Don't worry sweets, I enjoyed it."

Back at the table Nadine ordered a bottle of champagne. After it was gone Nadine looked at her watch. It was almost midnight.

"Time to call it an evening, gentleman. We need to get back to our husbands," Nadine said with a smile.

"What, you're married?" the men said in unison.

"Hey guys, don't tell me you hadn't noticed the rings on our fingers?" she said.

The ladies stood and thanked them for a fun evening and left the lounge. Casey was pretty wobbly on her feet.

"Let's check on your husband at the casino."

"Good idea," Casey slurred her words.

They searched the casino, but he was not there.

"Maybe he's in our cabin."

"Where is your cabin?" Nadine asked.

"Pearl deck, room 1056asshh," again slurring her words.

Casey opened her cabin room door, and there was her husband fully clothed lying sideways across the bed, passed out and snoring.

"What a wedding night, huh."

"Come on baby, let's have a night cap in my room."

"Okay, I love you" Casey said. Hugging Nadine and hanging onto her.

Nadine had a luxury suite with a mini bar and a king size bed. Casey sat on the edge of the bed and laid back. Nadine went to her closet and said, "I'm going to get into something more comfortable."

"So am I," Casey said. She got up and took her clothes off including her bra and panties. Nadine followed suit.

"God, you are one beautiful woman," Casey said staring at Nadine. Nadine pulled the covers back and they lay beside each other. Nadine was kissing and caressing Casey's nude body. Casey began to moan and move with Nadine's touch.

"Have you ever made love to another woman, Casey?"

"No, but I have fantasized about it many times. Are you going to make my fantasies come true?"

"Yes my dear, and mine also." Nadine placed her hand on Casey's breast.

38

Nadine awoke at 8:00 AM, Casey was gone. There was a note on the dresser.

My dear Nadine, I had a wonderful time last night. And what a great story I have to tell, about how I spent my wedding night making love with another woman. (LOL) Hope to see you again before the cruise is over, Love, Casey.

Nadine took a shower and put on her make-up. Her schedule for the day was breakfast in the main salon, then change into her bathing suit, lay by the pool, and get some morning sun. The ship was scheduled to dock in Ketchikan at 3:00 PM. Nadine wasn't going ashore. She figured it was just another tourist trap. The real beauty of Alaska lay ahead. She finished her bowl of fruit and juice and returned to her cabin to change into her bathing suit and robe, then headed for the main pool topside.

Nadine sat in a lounge chair at the edge of the pool listening to the soft music with a light breeze blowing from the west. A Bloody Mary rested in her right hand

and her sunglasses pinched the lower part of her nose.

This is the start of the good life, with so many adventures ahead.

———

Marcus had informed Frank that he was back running his business, and he wanted Frank to take over as the head of security, at least on a temporary basis or until Frank found a firm he could recommend. Frank thanked Marcus for the offer, but Frank liked his small investigative business. It allowed him the freedom to pick and choose what he wanted to do, and when he wanted to do it.

The first day back Marcus scheduled a meeting of all employees. When Marcus entered the meeting room, the employees stood and gave him a rousing applause.

"Thank you ladies and gentleman. It is good to be back in your presence. I want to let you know that my wife will be leaving the firm." Again, they stood and applauded with whistles and shouts. Marcus stopped and looked around the room. "Where is Max?" he asked. There was silence. Max's second in command stood and said, "We haven't seen or heard from him for two days."

"Find him and have him report to me immediately." The rest of the meeting was short, just general information to help Marcus catch up.

Max and Nadine both gone at the same time. Did Nadine

give Max the information to back off on his quest to kill me?

He called Frank. "Hi boss, how does it feel to be back in charge again?"

"To tell you the truth, Frank, I'm worried that maybe my dear wife didn't get around to telling Max about our divorce settlement. Max didn't show up this morning for the company meeting, and his second in command hasn't seen him for two days. Frank, see if you can find him."

"I'll do my best, Marcus," Frank said and they clicked off.

Knowing Nadine was on a cruise to Alaska, Marcus felt comfortable going to their home. He wanted to pick up additional clothes and other miscellaneous items. While there, he checked the secret room. Marcus could see the "Green Light" gun was missing along with the three-ring binder that held the altered disks. He went through a number of other things that they had stored there. He made a list of items that he would ask for prior to the divorce becoming final. Marcus had contacted an attorney a week earlier. He had him add the items to his list.

Marcus had a lock and key company come to the residence and the company building and change the locks on the entry and exit doors. The security codes were changed also.

He knew when she got back from her trip, she would be pissed, but by that time the divorce would be final.

He would allow her to come into the house and gather her belongings under his supervision, but under no circumstances would she be allowed into his home or business by herself.

Frank began his search for Max. He called the police and reported Max's company car stolen and gave them the license plate number. An hour later police called. The car had been found in Everett, Washington completely stripped. No sign of Max or any foul play. He buzzed Marcus and brought him up to date on Max's company car, and suggested Marcus turn it over to his insurance company.

39

It was 6:00 PM in Ketchikan. Three Chinese men were boarding at a security checkpoint on the ship. The security guard asked for their IDs and paper work. The guard checked their names against the workers manifest list, then waved them aboard.

They took the stairs to the top deck and followed the numbers until they reached Nadine's stateroom. One man knocked and waited. There wasn't any answer. They picked the lock with an electronic key-card and walked in. They placed their suitcases beside the bed and waited. The curtains leading to the patio deck were closed. One man peered out the glass slider to see how high the railing was, and if there were any security cameras.

Nadine's laptop computer and purse were sitting on the desk next to her make up. She had taken her credit card, electronic room card, and phone with her when she left to sun bathe.

Nadine was enjoying the sun and breeze off the water, when a man walked up to her and offered her one of the two Bloody Marys he had in his hands. She tipped her sunglasses up said, "Thank you, my good man."

"May I join you?" he asked sitting down before she could answer.

"That's what the chairs are for, I guess," she responded.

"My name is Mike Donaldson."

"Nice to meet you, Mr. Donaldson. I'm Nadine. Are you traveling alone?"

"No, my wife Casey and I are on our honeymoon."

"Oh, how wonderful." Nadine said with a smile.

"Well it's not that wonderful. I guess I screwed up last night. I played black jack at the casino and got very drunk. I don't remember getting back to our room at all. She won't even speak to me now."

"It seems you are in a bit of trouble," Nadine said.

"Casey said she made her own fun last night exploring new areas, I'm not sure what she meant. Maybe she was talking about the ship. Yeah, it must have been the ship."

He took a large tug on his Bloody Mary, and asked Nadine if she was traveling alone.

"No, I'm married, and he should be along in a few minutes."

"What do you think I should do or say to let her know that I'm sorry?"

"Maybe a nice souvenir from the cruise," Nadine answered.

"Yeah, like a t-shirt or something special to eat."

Nadine smiled broadly, "Yes, something special to eat." I know she'd enjoy that.

Mr. Donaldson picked up his drink and left, waving goodbye.

Nadine finished her Bloody Mary and headed for the snack bar that offered a variety of pizza slices. More and more people were using the pool now. It was a bit noisy for her.

The three men waiting for Nadine in her room spread out a map of the ship's security cameras locations and electrical grid. When it came time to dispose of Nadine's body, they would shut down the system for thirty seconds, long enough to take Nadine's body out on the patio and toss her overboard. One man would disable the cameras, and the other two would drop her over the side. There was a knock at Nadine's cabin door. The men inside were very quiet as one peered out the peephole in the door.

"It's a blonde woman," he whispered to the other two. They shook their heads and signaled with their hands not to answer the door. She knocked hard the next time, then gave up and walked away.

Casey walked to the nearest elevator and pushed the down button. When the doors opened Casey was face to face with Nadine. Casey got in and Nadine said, "Got time for coffee?"

"Yes, for you my dear, anytime."

They hugged before the elevator reached the main deck.

Nadine and Casey sat down at a table away from the crowd. A waitress took their order of coffee and returned almost immediately. Casey reached out and took Nadine's hand. Nadine noticed how warm it was and gave it a squeeze.

"I have to ask you something. Did you and I really make love last night, or did I just dream it?" Casey said hoping the answer would be true.

"Yes, we did honey, and it was wonderful."

"How do you feel about it now?" Nadine asked.

"I was a little drunk, and it was my first time with a woman but I would do it again with you in a heartbeat. What can I say, except it was the greatest sex I have ever had."

"I met your husband a couple of hours ago, and trust me he has no idea what had taken place last night," Nadine said." Both ladies laughed.

Casey said, "I hope we can see each other a couple more times before the cruise ends."

"I would enjoy that very much," Nadine answered with a gleam in her eye. The ladies exchanged cell phone numbers and headed for their separate rooms.

When Nadine placed the key card in the slot and opened her door, two men grabbed her and pushed her to the floor. They slapped tape on her mouth. She struggled but to no avail. The men bound her wrists behind her back. One man hit her in the stomach knocking the wind out of her. She curled into a ball and was making moaning sounds that were not audible. They lifted her to the bed, placing her in the middle. Another man hit her in the nose, breaking it, and causing profuse bleeding. Then they stopped and one said, "If I take the tape off your mouth, will you stay quiet?"

She nodded. He reached down and grabbed an end of the tape and ripped it off her mouth. He put his finger to his lips and shook his head.

"Who are you and what do you want with me?" she said nervously with tears running down her face, mixed with the blood from her nose.

"Your gun faulty, kill 24 Chinese. You pay back 50 million dollars or we kill you!" All the men spoke in broken English. The one who seemed to be in charge had Nadine's laptop in his hands. "Tell me how to get into offshore account." Nadine shook her head. The headman said something in Chinese to the others. One guy went to his suitcase and pulled out a large pair of electrical wire cutters and grabbed Nadine's hand. He held it tight and the other man put tape over her mouth again. The man with the cutters singled out her wedding ring finger and put the wire cutter over it and squeezed hard. Her finger snapped off quickly. The third man covered her hand with a towel. Nadine was screaming and struggling, but her sounds were muffled by the tape. The tape was removed again from her mouth. She was sobbing uncontrollably. He picked up her severed finger and said, "Very pretty rings missy, I give to wife." He smiled and removed the rings from Nadine's bloody finger.

"Now you tell me account number or more fingers gone," he said in broken English.

He grabbed another finger.

"No, please no," Nadine said looking at her hand without a ring finger. She started crying again.

"You be quiet or we kill you!" the man with the wire cutters said, looking very hostile.

"Alright, I'll tell you what you want to know. Turn on the lap top and put in the words Nasty Nadine." He was following her instructions.

"Now type, Yuke/pawn #8*u29722ldc@+50M.

A screen came up and asked for security code.

"What is security code?"

Nadine said, "Enter Minus/Marcus." The account opened, and the balance showed 55 million. He selected the button to transfer funds, put in an account number he had been given by the MSS, and entered the amount to be transferred. Another screen came up and said, please check all information before completing the transfer, then push "SEND". He did. A minute later his cell phone buzzed. The voice on the other end said, "Transfer completed," and clicked off.

The men began cutting Nadine's clothes off her body.

Soon she lay naked on the bed and the head man took pictures of her, proof of completing their mission.

They laid her on her stomach and taped her ankles together and pulled her feet up to her hands that were still taped behind her back. They taped her hands and legs together. Each of them beat her severely until she was unconscious.

One man opened his suitcase and pulled out a large, heavy-duty, black plastic bag and sliced several small slits in it. The men each worked the bag over Nadine's body until she was fully within. Then they pulled the top together and taped it shut.

At 3:00 AM the ship was quiet. When all was ready, they shut off all cabin lights. One man opened the curtains and slider to the patio. The electronics guy shut off the ships cameras and the other two men picked up and carried the bag that Nadine was in to the railing and dropped her overboard. They watched as the bag hit the water, then hurried back in just as the cameras came on again. The men pulled the bloody sheet and pillowcase from the bed, folded them neatly and placed them in one of their suitcases along with her shredded clothes. A man took out another waterproof bag and put Nadine's laptop, phone, finger, and purse in it and zipped it closed. The last thing in their suitcases was scuba gear and wet suits for each of them. Their plans were to go to the fantail with all three suitcases and change into wet suits, put on the scuba gear, slip into the water, and sink the three suitcases. The headman had the waterproof bag strapped to his wrist. A fishing boat that had been dogging the ship would be there to pick them up. All went as planned.

The MSS made two more attempts to recreate the deadly weapon. Each ended in failure and the loss of more lives. The MSS decided it was not worth the trouble and ended the experiments.

A week later what was left of Nadine's body washed up on shore near Petersburg, British Columbia. After an examination of the body, it was determined to be the remains of Nadine Radcliffe from Seattle, Washington. Her last known whereabouts was on a 10-day cruise to Alaska with the Princess cruise line. When it docked in Juneau, the ship's security went to Nadine's empty state room. It all appeared normal except that a sheet and pillowcase were missing. Her makeup was on the desk, and her clothes were hanging in the closet. And of course, the note from Casey was tucked in the side of her mirror. The ship's captain closed the gangways before anyone was allowed off the ship. A thorough investigation was underway. The Canadians notified the US authorities of Nadine's death, and they in turn notified her husband Marcus, who then called Frank Martini.

After a long discussion with Frank, Marcus called both attorneys handling the divorce and advised them about what had happened to Nadine. He asked to cancel the divorce settlement and send him the bill.

Even though he hated Nadine for what she had done, he was still shook up about her death and had no idea who could have committed such a horrible crime.

Ships security checked its registry for the name Casey. Only one was listed. They interviewed her and soon released her. She cried all the way back to her cabin.

40

Marcus contacted Jenny and asked her out for the weekend. She was very excited to hear from him and accepted the invitation. "How should I dress?" she asked.

"Maybe business casual and bring some extra clothes with you. It will be an overnight thing," he answered.

"What's going on?" she said with a giggle.

"All I'm telling you is, I want you to meet someone."

Marcus called Ben Swanson about Nadine's murder and Max being missing. He also mentioned how much he liked Jenny, and how their personalities clicked.

Ben offered to have them spend the weekend on the yacht with him. Marcus thought a minute, and then agreed. He was sure Jenny would enjoy it. Ben brought up the fact that he had also been seeing a new lady lately, and he would invite her to join them for the weekend.

"Perfect," Marcus said.

"Marcus, now that your problems with Nadine, Yuke and Max are over, do you still want the loan we discussed last week?"

"No Ben, I won't have to split up the company or pay off Nadine. Everything will be okay financially, but I do thank you for your generous offer. By the way, how is Hudson my favorite guard dog doing?"

"He's getting a little heavy. I should put him on a diet," Ben laughed.

"See you this weekend," Marcus said and clicked off.

Marcus drove to the B&B at 5:00 PM and picked up Jenny. They went to Jenny's place where she got her things for the weekend. She changed from her work uniform to a nice set of slacks, top, and tennis shoes. Then they headed south toward Bremerton Eagle Yacht Club.

Ben and his friend Stacey where waiting for them on the dock. After the introductions, the men carried the overnight bags to the yacht. Hudson was there to greet them, his tail wagging hard. Marcus put his and Jenny's bags in their cabin and joined the others on the deck. Stacey had opened a bottle of wine for her and Jenny. Ben and Marcus each had a beer. They still had a couple hours of daylight, and Ben wanted to take them on a short cruise. Stacey tended to the mooring lines, and Ben backed the yacht from the slip. They were lazily working their way up current. The ladies were deep in conversation.

The cruise was fun and lighthearted. The sun was beginning to fade and descend over the treetops, Ben headed back to the yacht club. The rest of the weekend was filled with beautiful sights and laughter. The ladies hit it off wonderfully. The couples made plans to get together again in a few weeks. Late Sunday morning Marcus and Jenny headed home. Marcus dropped Jenny off at the B&B to pick up her car.

"Sweetheart, I think it's time you give notice and come live with me," Marcus said.

Jenny didn't answer right away. She turned toward him, smiled a big broad smile, and threw her arms around his neck and said, "I was hoping you would ask me that. They kissed over and over. Marcus helped her put her things in her car and then drove back to his rental home.

Marcus was deep in thought about all the things that had happened to him over the past three and half months. Back to when he first met Frank in the steam room. And the many times Frank saved his life. He knew he wouldn't be alive today if it wasn't for Frank Martini.

The next day when Marcus was in his office, he sat at his desk and wrote out a check to Frank Martini for one million dollars. It covered his fees plus a hefty bonus. Marcus placed it in an envelope and put it in the top drawer of his desk. Marcus contacted Frank and requested they meet for lunch in the company's conference room.

Frank appeared precisely at 1:00 PM. Marcus was sitting at his desk.

"Frank, I want you to know how grateful I feel for your hard work and attention to me personally. I could not have weathered the storm of problems that we encountered during our time together without your help. I still have my life and my business thanks to you." He handed Frank the envelope, and sat back in his chair.

Frank looked at Marcus and said, "Boss, you're a hell of a man and a good friend."

Frank slowly opened the envelope and stared at the amount of the check inside.

"Holy crap!" Frank shouted with his eyes wide with delight. Marcus smiled and said, "You deserve it my friend." They shook hands and then hugged each other.

41

Frank nervously dialed a number, a receptionist answered sweetly, "Mega Data solutions, how may I help you?"

"May I speak to Ms. Diane Clark please?"

"Who may I say is calling, sir?"

"Please tell Ms. Clark, it's Roger Banister from Carmel California."

"One moment please."

Frank's throat was dry and his hands were shaking.

"Roger," Diane said. I have been thinking about you all day – how did you know?"

"I didn't Diane, but it's nice to know we were thinking along the same lines." They both laughed.

"How have you been for the last four months, traveling I suppose?" Diane said.

"A bit," Frank answered as if he wanted to change the subject.

"Is there anything wrong?" Diane asked.

"No, not at all. I was hoping you would be free next weekend and maybe we could meet at La Vista Carmel.

I secured the reservations in the event you were free. I have some very important information I would like to discuss with you."

I don't have anything on my schedule, Roger, and I would love to spend the weekend with you. That hotel and you have a very special spot in my heart," Diane sighed. "What time shall we meet?" She asked.

"Would 1:00 PM Friday be okay?"

"I'll see you then, lover," she laughed.

They hung up.

⬤◆●◆⬤

Frank's taxi pulled up in front of the hotel in Carmel. The weather was spectacular. He checked in early, in order to set up the room. Frank had flowers sent in and a bottle of champagne on ice. He went back to the lobby and awaited Diane's arrival. He had bought her a beautiful pearl ring. He wanted to wait on giving it to her, depending on her reaction to his truthful explanation of their previous meeting involving his undercover assignment of Nadine Radcliffe.

Frank had dressed in the same casual attire that he bought at the hotel four months ago. His plan was to have Diane get comfortable, have a drink before he told her his real name, and the purpose of his first visit to La Vista Carmel.

It wasn't long before Diane's taxi arrived. She looked stunning as she stepped from the taxi. Diane was wearing a bright yellow sundress and sandals. Her long beautiful blonde hair was pulled back in a ponytail. Frank walked out to greet her. They embraced and shared a friendly kiss.

"How have you been, Roger?" she said with a sincere interest.

"Well enough, and you?" he answered.

"I've been fine, just very busy with my company's work."

The taxi driver had unloaded her bags and was waiting for a tip. Frank handed him a fifty-dollar bill. The man smiled, hopped in his taxi, and left.

"I'll have the bellman take your things to the room while we share a drink on the lounge patio, if it's okay with you."

She nodded and they walked into the lounge and out to the adjoining patio. Frank pulled her chair out and she sat down. He couldn't take his eyes off her. Her beauty was so captivating.

"Still the consummate gentleman," she said touching his hand. "But somehow you seem a little different. What is the important information you need to discuss with me?"

"Too soon," Frank said.

The waiter appeared with their drink order.

"This weekend we are on our own, with no one to bother us, no meetings to attend or time schedule to adhere to," Diane sighed.

"God, it's good to see you again. You've been on my mind constantly," Frank said.

"That's such a nice thing to say, Roger, I have thought about you also." They picked up their drinks and walked hand in hand to the pool area, passing the beautiful gardens and flowers along the way.

"Here it is, a beautiful day on the weekend and not one soul using the pool," Frank said.

"Yes, I remember Roger, how much you enjoyed the pool," Diane said smiling.

There it is again, her calling me Roger. I have to quit putting it off any longer and tell her everything. And this setting is good enough.

"Let's find a comfortable seat, I need to talk to you," Frank whispered.

It was clear to Diane that he was uneasy with what he was about to say.

"Let me start at the beginning. When I met you, four months ago, I was not truthful with you. My name is not Roger Banister, it's Frank Martini."

Diane broke in, "I really had my doubts about your whole story, but at the time it didn't seem to matter that much."

"Yes, your intuition was right. I'm not a multi-millionaire either." Diane continued to listen with an unfriendly look.

"I'm a private investigator, and I was on the job."

"Oh, and what job would bring you to our annual

convention?" Diane questioned.

"I was hired by a husband to spy on his wife. He was suspicious of her activities in their co-owned business, and thought she may be selling company secrets to foreign governments or competitors."

"And did you?"

"Yes, I did."

"I don't suppose you will tell me the name of the woman involved and be truthful about it will you?"

"Yes, it was Nadine Radcliffe. I continued my investigation for the past four months. There were many twists and turns, involving murders, attempted murders, and the Chinese government."

"This is beginning to get very weird," Diane said easing her chair back from the table.

"I hope you believe me, because what I'm telling you is the truth."

"Okay, I'm still listening Roger, ah Frank, or whatever your name is. Is there more?"

"Yes, I'm afraid there is. Nadine and her husband had eventually settled on a divorce. While it was in the hands of the attorneys Nadine decided to take a cruise to Alaska. Around the first or second day on the water she was murdered."

Diane gasped! "Murdered. Oh my God, did you have anything to do with it?"

"Certainly not," Frank shot back. The Canadian and U.S. authorities are handling the investigation. So far three of the ship's crew are missing. They all are Chinese with false identifications. The authorities are trying to track them down.

"That's terrible," Diane said as a tear ran down her cheek.

"My part in this mess is over. I needed to get away and think of more pleasant things, and the most pleasant thing I could think of was you. I felt a need to clear up things between us. I'm desperately hoping you and I can still have that special feeling between us," Frank said with a longing look. Diane thought for a moment... "Frank, why don't you go to the room, I'll be there shortly. I need to be alone right now."

"I understand," Frank answered. He stood and excused himself then left.

Diane was more saddened by Nadine's sudden death, than Frank's deception.

As far as that goes I hadn't told him the truth either – the truth about my three marriages, and the many affairs during them. The truth that I didn't own the company. I'm the CEO. The truth that I was currently seeing someone. Frank is my lover, and I care for him deeply. And I want to continue seeing him.

"I'll tell him about my secrets sometime, but not right now. Now I want to spend the next few days making love with him." She left for the room in a much better mood.

Frank was sitting on the edge of the bed looking a bit

worried. Moments later Diane burst through the door, ran over to Frank, pushed him down on the bed, and jumped on top of him saying, "Get it out and get it up, because it's going for a ride."

They both struggled at taking off each other's clothes and laughed.

What a wonderful ride it was!

THE END

Coming in 2017!

R. T. Wiley keeps Frank Martini searching for answers in…

MARTINI 2

Springtime in Seattle has always been unpredictable. If you've lived in the northwest area for any length of time you should know that in planning an outdoor activity you should also have a plan "B" ready.

It was early morning and Jerry Golden had finished dressing for his daily run, except for putting on his new Nike Free 4.0 Fly-nit running shoes. He walked into the kitchen where his wife, Connie, was preparing breakfast for their two children. The smell of the bacon frying in the pan beckoned to him, but his will to lose a few additional pounds won him over. He gently kissed his wife on the cheek and walked to the front porch, sat down and put on his new running shoes.

Like any other athlete he constantly competed with himself to be faster and stronger. Maybe the shoes could help him shave a couple seconds off his fastest time. He ran the same route five days a week. You could set your clock by him.

A little cooler this morning, but not bad, he thought. Jerry checked his Garmin Forerunner 10 GPS watch and set it for the run. He stood and ran in place a few seconds then off he went. The shoes fit good and felt like they gave him an extra spring in his step. As he passed several different landmarks he could tell if he was ahead or behind his schedule.

At mile three he checked his watch. That can't be right. *I've shaved 18 seconds off my best time at this distance. I must be pushing myself harder than I thought.* "What else could it be?" he said with a satisfied smile on his face. "It's the shoes."

Jerry rounded the next corner where the trail went into the woods and then came a downhill stretch for a quarter of a mile. That ended at an old road that had been closed off to automobile traffic for years. The asphalt had weathered badly and the large cracks allowed tall thick weeds to grow in them, they appeared everywhere. Mother Nature was slowly taking over what man had made.

There was a rusty, old, abandoned delivery truck, minus the wheels, just off the edge of the road. Its paint had long ago faded with age and the writing on the sides was now unreadable. The old truck had been there for as long as he could remember. Jerry had never seen anyone around it. Except today. He saw movement.

He didn't want to break his stride and slow down, but with a glance to the right, he saw a man sitting in the driver's seat tossing a Raggedy-Ann doll in the air. He heard a small child's voice saying, "Give it back mister!"

"Damn," he was doing so well on his time. Jerry didn't want to stop, but he had this awful gut feeling, something seemed to be terribly wrong.

Somewhat winded, he walked slowly over to the truck and saw a little girl with curly blonde hair sobbing. The man said, "Stop crying, you little bitch!" and the man pointed a gun at her head.

"Wait, wait!" Jerry shouted, standing just a few feet from the driver's window of the delivery truck. Jerry raised his arms to his shoulders and extended them out toward the man sitting in the truck's driver's seat.

The man swung around, pointed the gun at Jerry and pulled the trigger. The bullet hit Jerry in the chest, he staggered and fell face forward, hitting the ground hard then lay motionless.

The man grabbed the little girl and took off running for the woods. Her screams echoed off the trees and then became silent. Jerry lived long enough to write the words, child, truck, and doll, in his own blood before he died.

A couple of hours later, knowing he was long overdue, his wife Connie, called the police fearing something bad had happened to him.

It wasn't long after her call that they had organized a search party. They found Jerry's body and his message. One of the cops at the scene called for the homicide team. There was always someone at the news organizations that monitored the police frequency to get a jump on a story. Soon a news chopper was hovering over the crime scene and reporters gathered below.

"Child, truck, doll," The detective on scene said. "There's no child. That just leaves the truck and the doll." The detective walked to the truck and found the first clue. A Raggedy Ann doll. He placed it in an evidence bag and tagged it. The detective knew that with the lack of anymore evidence, this case would wind up in the cold case files in a hurry.

Clouds were forming, the weather was about to change. The police had finished their on scene investigation. The medical examiner had loaded the body into his wagon and started off for his office in downtown Seattle. During the investigation no shell casing were found. The detectives figured the shooter must have used a revolver. It began to rain, and Jerry's dried blood was soon loosened and washed away. Only the pictures that were taken by the police forensic team remained to remind them of what Jerry wrote before his death. It rained hard the rest of the day and far into the night. A grieving family had no answers, and neither did the police. They processed the Raggedy-Ann for DNA and fingerprints. Nothing of value came back.

The murder didn't make the front page, it was relegated to the less important news on page four, on the bottom of the fold. Not that it wasn't newsworthy, it was just stories like that hurt the city's tourism business, and with the economy in the dumps, the city needed all the help it could get to keep the tourism business alive.

———◆◆◆◆———

The weather reports for the next few days said it was going to be beautiful, warm and sunny. Frank Martini had gathered up his beach attire and headed out to his favorite spot on the beach near the pier. He felt his pale body was in need of some color and he always enjoyed the female scenery there.

Frank's case with the Radcliffe's had finally come to an end and his private investigating business was flourishing. Marcus Radcliffe was eternally grateful for the outcome and paid Frank a cool million dollars for his involvement. Frank had moved his office to an up-scale business location, and his part time sidekick Tommy Saliman was happy to be making a few bucks to add to his Seattle PD retirement. Frank had a weekend with Diane Clark in Carmel and patched things up between them.

Martini pulled into a parking place close to the pier. It was early and there were plenty of good spots left on the beach. He picked up the daily newspaper from the newsstand right in front of his parking place. He had a bag full of beach items, a shorty beach chair, towel and his cooler. He tucked the paper under his arm, grabbed the rest of his stuff and walked toward the water until he found the spot he wanted.

He placed his chair precisely at the right angle to take full advantage of the sun. He sat down, adjusted his straw hat, put on his sunglasses and reached into his cooler for a beer. Yeah, it was a little early to start drinking but Frank was a cool guy and he really didn't have to answer to anyone. No wife, no kids. He stretched out, unfolded the paper and relaxed. When he got to page four, he read the relatively short piece on the murder of Jerry Golden. Frank stopped and thought a minute. He neatly folded the edges of the article and carefully tore them from the paper and put them in his bag.

ACKNOWLEDGMENTS

To my wife Marilyn for her continued support and help and checking my work.

To Sally Kennedy for coming to my rescue.

To Debbie Lewis for bringing it all together.

To Larry Tyree and Mike Konyu, my friends and aspiring authors.

And to all my former law enforcement friends for their support.

THANK YOU!

ABOUT THE AUTHOR

Former police officer and author R. T. Wiley brings over a decade's of experience in law enforcement to his writing. From an urban police department in California to a county sheriff's department in Oregon, Wiley draws on his adventures in the Pacific Northwest. Now retired, he resides in Chandler, Arizona with his wife Marilyn and their dog Hudson.

Made in the USA
Columbia, SC
17 March 2020

89222914R00146